One Dead Marine

A Savage Soul Scorched Earth™ Novel

John Knotts

DEDICATION

This book is dedicated to The Skippers.
You know who you are
and you know why this is dedicated to you.

Also, to Bogo, for without his efforts, none of this
would be possible.

CONTENTS

PREFACE

Scorched Earth™

One Dead Marine

The advanced society of the twenty-first century died a painful death--and the killer's name was Yellow Mike.

In January 2045, this strange viral agent made its presence known almost simultaneously in several of the world's largest cities. As doctors watched helplessly, Yellow Mike corrupted the DNA of its victims. In the early stages, subtle endocrine changes resulted in thought disorders and paranoia. In the later stages, the pain of tumors, dermatological conditions, and digestive problems seemed to defy treatment by even the most advanced painkillers. Yellow Mike was not 100% fatal--but no one ever fully recovered from its effects. Rather, the fortunate few who did survive were permanently altered at the genetic level.

Within days of the first reported deaths, the Internet was abuzz with promises of immunizations and cures. To feed the insatiable demand for any shred of hope, dimensional transporters operated at capacity and pharmaceutical couriers from all over the world raced to deliver "miracle drugs" to communities willing to pay anything. Some of these treatments were mere placebos--but many were legitimate experimental agents, the goal of which was to modify a subject's DNA, before Yellow Mike got the chance. There was no time for testing--but there were plenty of willing test subjects, and the world's governments were powerless to control the massive flow of new drugs. Entire communities inoculated themselves with various experimental gene-altering agents. Sometimes, the effects were almost as bad as Yellow Mike. Sometimes they weren't, but few of the agents proved effective as Yellow Mike continued to spread.

Some communities and families chose another option, draining their savings to build airtight, underground shelters, some capable of sustaining life for more than a century. Still others opted for cryogenic stasis, hoping to awaken in a world where Yellow Mike was a distant memory.

For those outside the shelters and sleeper pods, fear covered the dying Earth like a thick stew. Stores, warehouses, and armories were looted and left in shambles by hordes of the desperate and the mad. Military and police forces operated on skeleton crews. Their efforts to maintain order were often valiant--but ultimately futile.

As madness spread through the highest levels of world government, long time enemies exhausted their remaining military forces on suicide assaults. At the direction of paranoid leaders, almost every nation bypassed the manual safeguards of their nuclear arsenals. There weren't enough healthy people left to man the silos and those that remained could not be trusted.

On August 15, 2045, the first set of missiles launched and virtually every other missile in the world launched in response. Nuclear fire gave way to nuclear winter and the world, as anyone had known it, was gone forever.

One Dead Marine

For those in the strongest shelters, when communications with the outside world went silent, life became a matter of dismal survival. For generations people lived and died in the shelters, hoping their children or grandchildren might one day watch a sunrise.

Outside, those who had survived both Yellow Mike and the Great Destruction faced yet another horror--a strange new virus commonly believed to be a mutation of Yellow Mike. Unlike its predecessor, however, this new virus did not target the living. Rather, it had the mysterious and terrifying effect of altering and reactivating the central nervous systems of the recently deceased. All around the world, corpses began rising as mindless, flesh-eating zombies, and the burnt ruins of once thriving population centers swarmed with armies of living dead. Nonetheless, in the wilderness, in caves, and in fortress-like compounds, the heartiest human survivors adapted, pressed on, and dug in expecting a new ice age.

But the legacy of Yellow Mike had just begun to unfold. The first generation of human children born after the Great Destruction immediately showed the effects of genetic corruption. Mutations ranged from the barely perceptible, to the nightmarish, to the incredible--with entire populations often bearing no resemblance to their parents or even to the species homo sapiens. Over time, these sons and daughters of Yellow Mike ventured back into the world and made it their own. They stripped the accessible ruins and tore down even the skeletons of mighty skyscrapers for crude building materials. As the sky finally cleared and the earth began to warm, new towns and cities rose from the rubble and a new world was born.

With times so hard, the influence of the divine and the demonic became more tangible. Priests and witches found themselves able to perform miraculous feats, almost at will. At the same time, dabblers experimented with the arcane and found that the new world was rich with magic, blurring the line between the possible and impossible.

But even aside from the magic, this world was not like the old. The monsters and zombies that seemed to lurk in every shadow, the ruthless raiders that seemed to roam every highway, and the prejudice between the new species of humankind seemed to ensure each community's isolation. The relics of the old world could simultaneously make a man a god and a target. They were sought and hoarded by many--shunned and rejected by others.

It is a world of science and magic, of men and monsters, of peace and war, of unspeakable wonders and sudden, violent death. It is a world where a man can as soon become a hero as become a memory.

PROLOGUE

Anthony Moon -- American Marine

One Dead Marine

Born on 15 Jun 2025, Anthony (Tony) Moon was an American Indian most recently from Aurora, Colorado, a suburb of Denver.

Tony's childhood was relatively normal, but he pretty much lived the life of a military brat. His grandfather was enlisted in the Army--he was killed when a car bomb went off at a checkpoint in the city of Kirkuk, Iraq, during Operation Iraqi Freedom. His father was a pilot in the Air Force and retired from Colorado Springs, Colorado, and from there he moved his family to the suburbs of Denver.

Tony graduated from Gateway High School, top in his class, and completed an Associate's Degree in Liberal Arts, through the Community College of Aurora. At the age of 20, he chose to enlist in the United States Marine Corps, to follow in the military footsteps of the men in his family.

In Marine Basic Training, Moon was cited for his outstanding performance during The Crucible, the final endurance test of teamwork before graduation. He choose to go into the Combat Arms--Infantry--due to his strong desire to support the United States' ongoing fight against terrorism. Due to his previous college experience, he was immediately promoted, out of basic training, to the rank of Lance Corporal.

The Corps instantly noticed Corporal Moon's potential and he was hand-selected for follow-on training in Force Recon. During the months of his final training, Yellow Mike emerged across the planet in the world's largest cities. After completing a very rushed course in Recon, Moon was sent immediately to New York City to join up with a Recon Battalion sent there to restore order to the city now under Martial Law. A large percentage of the population had already died, and another large population was currently experiencing Yellow Mike's madness. As a result, the city was in a state of chaos and things looked pretty hopeless.

As the Corporal's troop transport traveled into the city toward Battalion HQ, the lead vehicle was hit by some kind of explosion. Suddenly gunfire erupted around the convoy and all the Marines that lived through the initial assault evacuated the vehicles.

Unfortunately, some of the commanders were concerned about the possible effects of the Yellow Mike on the enlisted and all the weapons and equipment were under guard in the center convoy vehicle. It seemed that several members of the military had suddenly just started shooting their fellow Marines without reason as of late.

Just as Tony started to make his way to the convoy's supply truck, the vehicle disintegrated in a fiery explosion, taking out the equipment and Convoy Commander, a Major in Recon. In the pandemonium, a Gunnery Sergeant took semi-control of the situation and ordered the remainder of survivors to break up, slip into the buildings around them, and rendezvous back at HQ.

Keeping mostly off the streets and to himself, Tony finally made it to HQ to find what looked more like a fire base in the jungles of a foreign country than an office complex in New York City. Tired, dirty, and armed only with his Bush pocketknife, he was allowed in the compound ready to provide his report to the officer in charge.

   Here, he stepped through the gates of Hell, his first real assignment as a Marine, and to his mind, came a saying he learned in training, "Ye, thou I walk through the valley of the shadow of death, I will fear no evil, for I am the baddest mother fucker in the valley." Today he didn't feel all that bad...to that he shrugged his shoulders and whispered to himself, "Semper Fi, do or die!" With that, he made his way for the battalion headquarters.

1

NEW YORK CITY -- 2045

These pages chronicle my life as a Marine and whatever should follow. Should you read these items, may they amuse and amaze you--if they don't, then throw them away.

~ Tony Moon

One Dead Marine

Well, nobody ever said the Marines would be a boring job! If they had looked into my future, they sure wouldn't have said that about me either.

This journal is the record of my life as a Marine in the United States of America. If you have found it, either it's been lost or I'm dead--in either case, enjoy.

Day one of my first assignment turned into my last day in 2045...yes, you heard me right...my last day in the year 2045.

I hooked up with Private First Class Ruiz at the battalion headquarters in New York City and we were attached to a Marine Captain named Landry for our first mission into downtown. We were going to a nearby public transporter to do something, but no one gave us any more details than that--they never told the low-ranking troops anything anyways.

We didn't encounter any resistance on the way to the transporter station, but we could hear sporadic gunfire all over the place on the nearby streets. The entire patrol was clearly wound tighter than industrial springs.

Ruiz didn't seem to mind; however, he actually looked like he was enjoying the whole damn thing. Me on the other hand, I was nervous as shit. I kept expecting some crazy son-of-a-bitch to jump out and start shooting us, but it didn't happen.

New York City -- 2045

When we made it to the transporter station, we processed through to Water and Fulton Street near Wall Street downtown.

Those transporters gave me the willies. The whole dimensional power and dimensional transporter thing was never really my bag in school. About ten years after I was born, some guy named Torgler discovered a series of alternate dimensions. His big claim to fame was finding one that was a source of unlimited energy and, after several years it powered practically everything on the plant--well used to.

Soon after that discovery by Torgler, researchers found a way to use one of the other dimensions he discovered to move people from one spot on Earth to another. The shit was way above my head--I was a Marine after all, remember?

Just as we got out of the transporter, the captain got a call on his radio telling him to bring the patrol back to battalion headquarters. He ordered Ruiz and I to sit tight and wait for them to return. "Don't get in trouble," he said. Right, what kind of trouble can two green-ass Marines get into in the middle of New York City?

Have you ever heard the saying, "the calm before the storm?" Well, it was pretty quiet at the station so Ruiz and I made ourselves at home in the lounge and waited. Ruiz quickly found some cartoons on the tube and I had just picked up a daily Times news disk, when my radio went off.

It was the captain and he wanted us two--yea, just the two of us--to go get some woman at some Heliogistics corporate headquarters building. He told us the building was located at the corner of Williams and Waters, but I didn't even know where we were, let alone where the corner of Williams and Waters was located.

The lady's name we were ordered to pick up was Jessica Westgate and we were supposed to bring her back to battalion headquarters "ASAP."

The mission seemed simple enough until you figure the whole city had gone crazy and just about everyone out there wanted to kill anything that moved.

We obtained some quick directions from a local map on the station wall and I planned a secondary route through the subway system just in case our original route got compromised.

Setting out, I put Private Ruiz on point--he was a good kid, but definitely not Recon material. Aside from a run in with a group of scared businessmen, the streets were relatively quiet.

We did see one guy in an alley who looked dead, but we had our orders and didn't have time to check him out--it probably was a trap anyway...God, that place was crazy!

We arrived at the corporate building and no one was there--everything looked pretty tame.

When we went in, we found that the building had a special security system in place that controlled entry--a pretty foolproof system that I remembered from my Marine training.

The security system was designed to prevent entry into the building past the lobby if you were carrying any weapons. Since we were both loaded up, that meant us.

Checking out a magazine on Heliogistics in the lobby, I figured out this company was the one responsible for the development and manufacture of pulse weapon technology. I was thinking to myself that maybe this lady might be important to the military because of that, but the whole thing was way over my pay grade.

Using the phone in the lobby and the building directory, I was able to ring up this Westgate chick to try to get her to come down stairs and meet us. She started immediately ranting about something to do with Bradley's cure and then hung up on me. I tried calling her back several times, but she wouldn't answer the damn phone again.

At this point, I was pretty worried this crazy Yellow Mike disease had affected her too, but we had our orders.

I tried to bypass the security system, but failed, so I called the captain to check in. Of course he wasn't concerned as to whether this Westgate woman wanted to go or not and simply repeated his orders--as if I would have forgotten them by now.

Finally, I decided to leave Ruiz in the lobby with our weapons. I didn't want to leave our guns just lying around some office lobby so some Yellow Mike crazy could get at them.

As I entered the elevator area, I ran into four businessmen fleeing the building. I think they were more scared of me then I was of them. I got a key card from one of them that allowed access to the floor Mrs. Westgate was on and they split. Just as they were leaving; however, one of them told me that this woman shouldn't even be in the building.

I was a bit suspicious of those men, but I had to file it away with all the other useless garbage that was in my mind at the time and press on.

I took the elevator up to the fifth floor--according to the directory, her office was room 551--and headed straight for her door.

On my way to room 551, an explosion on one of the lower levels rocked the building. It felt like an earthquake on the fifth floor and literally knocked me off my feet.

Immediately I thought of Ruiz sitting downstairs in the lobby, but I knew I didn't have time to worry about him.

With a renewed sense of motivation, I proceeded quickly to find Westgate's office. When I opened the door to her office I saw two things. First off, I noted that she was an extremely attractive looking woman. That was when my eyes focused down the barrel of a small semi-automatic pistol pointed directly at my head--the second thing.

After a little Marine charm, I convinced Mrs. Westgate that I didn't know anything about some guy named Bradley and I was just some stupid flunky doing his government-directed job.

The entire time I was trying to reason with her, she was going off about this guy named Bradley and his cure, but finally she started to believe me enough so we could try to leave.

By the time I sweet-talked her into leaving, the building fire alarms had gone off and the stairwell and elevators had shut down--damn computer-driven buildings.

Mrs. Westgate showed me another way out of the building--an alternate route--which led down a ladder on the outside of the building.

She was checking out the ladder when I finally was able to use the phone to call downstairs and check on Ruiz--of course the system was disconnected.

The escape route this woman pointed out to me took us down the outside of the building on a fire escape ladder. As we were about to head down the ladder, the building's first floor windows exploded outwards and the flames from within burst out the shattered windows and started licking their way up the ladder towards us.

That was when I noticed a cable that was connected to the building at about the third floor that we might be able to use. The cable connected to a telephone pole across the street. I soaked a couple of drapes and quickly covered ourselves so the heat wouldn't get to us. We climbed down the ladder to the third floor and slid across the street on the cable.

I had Jessica hold onto me as we slid across the street on the angled cable and that was pretty cool!

Suddenly there was a thunderclap--a sound I would not like to ever hear again. The Heliogistics building started to collapse due to the damage on its first floor. I did a quick scan for Ruiz as we scrambled for cover, but couldn't find him anywhere. If the explosion was that sudden, he probably never stood a chance.

As the building crumbled around us and dust and heat washed into the alley we were finding cover in, I couldn't help but wonder if those four men had something to do with the explosion.

As if that wasn't bad enough, just then the civil defense sirens started going off. All I could think of at that moment was, "Shit, New York is under attack!"

Over loud speakers in the city, we could hear announcements that they would seal the shelters in ten minutes. There I was, stuck in downtown New York City with a beautiful crazy woman and following orders to do something I had no clue about--it just wasn't my day.

We immediately started to move--we had to get somewhere safe. It was just about then that some whacked-out, Yellow Mike victim popped out of an alley and started shooting at us. I was thinking at this point that this day would never end.

I emptied Jessica's peashooter at the guy and finally took him down with none other than my trusty Bush pocket knife my dad gave me on my 15th birthday.

Unfortunately, in the gunfight, the guy blew a chunk out of my shoulder before he went down and man did that hurt. I think a grim smile covered my face when I considered if I would get a Purple Heart for that.

I turned to grab Jessica and saw that that crazy fool had shot her too! I did a quick patch job on her and she whispered something about using the transporter with a key card that she slid into my hand. The last thing she breathed, before she passed out, was to use the current year as the pass code.

At that moment, I left all stealth behind. I threw her over my good shoulder, grabbed the other guy's weapon lying in the street, and made a beeline for the transporter station. It wasn't easy with one busted up shoulder, let me tell you.

When we arrived at the station, it was a mad house-- it looked like the return line at Best Buy the day after Christmas!

Again, I had to employ my Marine charm. The crowd recognized my authority--and loud voice--and parted like the Red Sea. This was great, because I had no idea what else I would have done if they hadn't moved aside. As I was surging through the parting crowd, I enlisted the aid of some security guard--I think it actually made his day that he was helping a U.S. Marine.

One Dead Marine

As I arrived at the transport pedestal, I bumped past this one black guy who wouldn't move. He kept giving me a rash of shit about taking too long on the transporter. He was pretty annoying while I was trying to figure out how to operate the system, but he didn't attack me or anything, which was a relief.

On the pad, after a little trial and error, I punched in the correct code, inserted the keycard, and entered the pin, which I suspected to be the current year as Jessica had told me.

The next thing I knew, we were in a small circular room--some type of stasis capsule I gathered from the look of it.

When Yellow Mike was first discovered a year ago, the rage over cryogenics grew to epic proportions. I had heard of these places around the world, but had never seen one before. It was pretty clear to me that was where we were.

There were three cryogenic tubes in the small room and a console in the center of the wall across from the tubes. One of the tubes already had someone in it. My mind was a bit hazy from the pain, but I made sure I put Mrs. Westgate in one of the tubes and I got in the other.

My tube closed and I heard a release of air.

2

WELCOME TO HOLLYWOOD

Sometimes there is a fine line between reality and fantasy; however, then that fantasy is so distorted, yet actually real, that's where the fun begins.

~ Tony Moon

Next thing I know, the tube was reopening and my arm still hurt like Hell!

Ok, that was day one of my New York City duty--oh, 150 years ago! Seems we were sleeping for about that long, but I didn't find out that until much later.

I crawled around in the dark of the stasis capsule for a little bit until I could find an emergency light source. In the dim glow of the emergency lights, I could make out mine and the other two cryogenic tubes.

Jessica was still frozen in her tube, but in the muted light I could make out that the third tube in the capsule had failed somehow and the guy in it was long dead. His wallet identified him as Rick Jackson. I took a lighter off his skeletal corpse, but that was about it in the room.

As I inspected the capsule, I determined that the main power generator on the pod had failed and the battery backup was only enough to unfreeze me. The battery backup was dying and I couldn't get Jessica out because there wasn't enough power. It seemed that I was going to have to go get help.

There was a hatch at the top of a ladder on the roof of the pod. Opening that hatch lead into a tunnel leading straight up. At the top of the tunnel was another hatch, but this one was sealed shut and there wasn't any obvious way to unlock it.

I finally figured out that it was some kind of an explosive hatch, but there wasn't enough power in the system to blow it open from the control panel. After some trial and error, I was able to rig the explosive hatch to blow.

The room above me was pretty dark, but I could make out some ambient light, like it was nighttime. I started to climb out of the hatch and I saw two people in the room above me. They were kind of odd--just standing there, not moving and staring at nothing.

Just when I thought they were store mannequins or something, one of them shambled over to me in the dark and reached out for me. I couldn't make out much in the dark, but whatever it was, it was really scary looking. At that point I was thinking it might be have been another victim of Yellow Mike, so I scrambled back down into the capsule. I waited, but it didn't follow me.

My shoulder was still in pain and I could tell the blow from that guy's gun had dislocated it. I gave my best attempt at resetting it, which caused me to black out for a little while.

When I woke, I reviewed all my available options. Seeing really only one, I decided to waste the two guys upstairs. The problem was, the best weapon I had now was a club since both of the guns I had were out of ammo.

Timing my attack, I sprang up into the room to pummel this guy. That was when I realized this was certainly no normal man I was dealing with. He looked like something right out of that 1970's horror classic, Night of the Living Dead.

I hit the thing once and I could tell it was pretty stupid when it fought--it didn't even attempt to block or dodge, but holy shit was it strong. It grabbed hold of me and bit me on the neck with such force that I blacked out again.

I woke up back on the bottom of the floor of the stasis pod. I figured I must have fell backwards through the open hatch when it attacked me--that probably saved my life.

At this point the world was spinning and I was in tremendous pain. I'm not sure how long I had passed out, but the battery fueling Jessica's pod was really dying by the time I came to. I decided I had to get some replacement power from somewhere quickly.

What doesn't kill a Marine just makes him stronger--right?

I climbed back up the ladder again and there it was just silently waiting for me. This time, by luck, I was able to club it to death. I say, "to death," but really the guy was already dead once. I found that hitting him in the head did the trick--hitting him anywhere else pretty much had no effect.

This guy's mate shuffled over and I planned to give her the what for, but no dice. I would guess it would have been lights out for me when suddenly she--or it--simply slumped to the ground.

Standing behind her--my savior--was this rather filthy guy digging a huge axe out of the back of her cranium. This guy was pretty insistent that I go with him immediately. Sure enough it was good thinking because there were more of these slow-moving monstrosities milling around.

Once I got out of the building I was in, it turned out our stasis chamber was under the kitchen floor of a house in a subdivision. I was thinking that maybe the pod belonged to that dead guy in the other tube.

The subdivision was all ruined and overgrown with jungle everywhere. My rescuer said something about it being Hollywood and I was surprised that we ended up in California.

*****

Once we got away from the housing area, this guy felt we were pretty safe and we holed up by a river. He told me his name was Jack Luster and he was a scavenger. After we talked for a little bit, I discovered that Jessica and I had slept for about 150 years after some "Great Destruction." That would explain the civil defense sirens in New York.

Jack also set me straight that we weren't in California, but actually in Hollywood, Florida--near Miami. I had never been to Florida before, so I figured I was just as lost there as when I was in New York City.

Jack explained to me that there were two major groups in the area. The Fool had some stronghold in Miami and he hated something Jack referred to as Shelties and Sleepers. Turns out I was what they refer to as a Sleeper--someone who had come out of a stasis pod like I did.

Jack also talked about this place called Homestead, but didn't tell me anything about it. None of this sounded promising; my head still swam with pain, I was exhausted, and everything seemed just too unreal.

Once Jack found out what my name was, he got all animated. It would seem that he knew me--or at least my name-- but that didn't seem possible or make any sense.

When Jack discovered that I was also a sleeper, he really got excited--scary excited. It was then that he told me that we had to go see his boss. He did warn me to stay away from some outpost near where we were because the people there work for the Fool and they would kill me because I was a sleeper.

At this point, I really didn't trust this guy, but I also didn't see anyone else to turn to. I informed him that we had to get another power source to wake Jessica up in the sleeper capsule. He told me that his boss would be able to help--again, I just didn't trust him.

Then Jack said something really strange--he said his boss knows magic. This guy was either crazy, or people have learned how to wield powers that seem like magic or something. I considered everything that had happened up to now and at least surmised that this magic Jack was referring to might be an after effect of Yellow Mike, radiation, or something similar.

Jack let me sleep a little and then we made our way to his boss' camp. When we arrived there, he wanted me to wait outside the camp while he went in alone. I suspected he didn't want me to be warned as to what was really going on. He used the excuse that the people in the camp might attack me, but I didn't believe him.

When he left, I moved to another location in the woods to watch him. Jack went straight to the center tent of the encampment. A little bit later he came out looking for me. Not finding me, he looked really worried and returned to the main tent.

I would assume that his boss was pretty pissed off when he returned empty-handed because, as I was sitting there hidden in the woods watching the tent, Jack's head came rolling out without the rest of his body. What a nightmare that was to see!

I was pretty horrified at that point, but I couldn't stop watching that large central tent. That was when this thing came out of the tent. He looked like a huge burnt red man with a face made up of all odd angles; however, he had an oddly regal appearance. Whatever he was, he started barking out some orders to go look for me and then he pulled out this odd glass globe and started concentrating on it.

I had this really weird and scary feeling for a second. It was then that I decided to split.

*****

I made my way to some lake and then I followed along the shore of it. I came across this guy on some type of hover bike. I kind of took him by surprise, but he turned out to be pretty cool.

I was able to convince him to help me--maybe because I could barely stand at that point. This guy seemed nice enough, not knowing who I was and all. He introduced himself as Leadhead, but this time I gave a fictitious name.

We headed in a direction away from that awful camp and the weird burnt man. Leadhead took me on a wild ride on his bike, which I found really pretty awesome, even in my pain-induced delirium.

After awhile, we stopped and rested for a bit--I needed that. Sitting around a campfire, Leadhead filled me in on some other things about the area that Jack hadn't told me.

The first thing he told me was that he worked at the outpost that Jack had mentioned earlier--the one that was supposed to be aligned to the Fool. Leadhead confirmed for me that the Fool did hate shelties, which were people who live in shelters, and sleepers--like me. I kept the fact that I was a sleeper a secret.

The place Jack referred to as Homestead was actually an old Air Force Base at one time and it was where sleepers and shelties had come together and had grown in size and power over the years.

The Fool and Homestead engaged in some kind of a war of sorts. That made sense, since the Fool hated shelties and sleepers and that was what lived at Homestead.

Leadhead told me that Homestead was working to restore order to the area and the Fool loved the anarchy. I was thinking to myself that I should meet up with the people from Homestead and help them.

After resting a bit, Leadhead stashed his hover bike by a river and started to lead me to the outpost on foot. As we walked towards the outpost, I stumbled on something metal jutting out from the undergrowth. I kept quiet about what I stumbled on, and convinced Leadhead to go on ahead while I tied my boot.

It turned out, right there near their outpost and hidden under the vines, was a hatch entrance. After a quick investigation, I could tell it was a hatch to a stasis pod like the one I was in.

I messed with the locking mechanism and I was able to get inside to examine the pod. Down under ground and inside the chamber, it looked just like the one I was in. Two of the cryogenics tubes were damaged like Rick Jackson's and the residents inside were dead. Upon searching them, they each had a small caliber pistol on them.

The remaining functioning tube held a rather attractive young girl in stasis. I tried to pull her from her sleep, but the computer required a logon and my meager hacking skills were no match for it.

What I did find; however, was her generator was still working just fine, so I pulled the backup battery and planned to come back to try to get her out later.

Before leaving the pod, I also stripped out the explosive charge in the hatch, which was a big piece of

C4. I figured I could probably find a use for it later. On my way to catching up to Leadhead, I stashed the heavy backup battery along the trail in the bushes with hopes of picking it up later.

I caught up with Leadhead before he reached the outpost so that I could enter with him. Just outside the outpost, I stopped to do a little trading with a wrinkled old guy named Smitty. He seemed to like me, but he probably took me to the cleaners on my trade.

In this day and age, people used credit to barter in a fairly efficient, but probably one-sided system. They did have precious metal coins that they used for currency--essentially 10 grams of metal was equal to a coin. These coins came in copper, silver, gold, and platinum. This was definitely different to the credit system I was familiar with 150 years ago.

I got some coins from Smitty for the C4 and made my way into the compound with Leadhead.

Leadhead took me to meet with the outpost's leader, who name was Throm Burlash. The nightmare continued when I met him because Throm was some kind of mutated monster or something. He was huge and his thick skin was all green and brown. They guy also had these crazy big sharp teeth that looked incredibly scary.

Although scary looking, this guy was pretty reasonable. Throm told me that practically everyone at the outpost worked for a woman named Regan. Regan was some kind of lieutenant to the Fool back in Miami.

Looking to ingratiate myself with the indigenous people, I convinced this monster to let me prove myself and become one of "Regan's soldiers." Heck, I already had the uniform, so why not, right? This deal allowed me to safely use the resources at the outpost while I figured out what to do about Jessica and this other sleeper woman I found.

Being able to travel freely in the outpost, I was able to get a good look around. I inquired about a doctor, which led me to this mysterious old woman.

The best I can describe her was a witch, but for some reason she took a liking to me--Marine charm again I figured. The rest of the coins I picked up for trading the C4 went to this old woman. She had a bizarre ability to heal people--some people called it this magic I had heard about, but I really wasn't sure what to make of it. Needless, she didn't use any medical skills or equipment I was familiar with.

After spending a little time with the old woman, I started to call her Grandma. She healed my dislocated shoulder and fixed up my wounds, but I didn't have enough to pay for it all. Grandma told me she would, "Expend all her magic on me anyway," with the promise that I would pay her back. I owed that kindly old hag what amounted to a tidy sum and planned fully to pay her back somehow.

I determined then that I really needed to learn how to survive better financially in this new world; even if it killed me to do so.

One Dead Marine

All healed up and knowing that I needed to get out of this camp quick, I tried to lift Leadhead's hover bike key while he was sleeping, but he caught me. I was able to talk my way out of it though and the next day, I talked him into going with me to get a "Sleeper Chick" out of stasis. I figured this would be a good way to get his help and at some point I would be able to dump him.

Leadhead got pretty excited because it would appear there were pretty large bounties on sleepers offered by the Fool, so he took me to talk to Throm about it. Throm was also really excited about the concept and said he would pay us a hefty sum if we did that for him.

Burlash told me about this sick ritual the Fool had with sleeper women. I know I would never want to see it, but he told me they send the women down this slide into an area full of zombies in Miami. These zombies were in fact the same thing I ran into when I tried to leave the stasis chamber in Hollywood.

I didn't tell them about the stasis chamber right near their outpost, even though it would've made me pretty rich at that point. I just couldn't see having that crazy ritual done to anyone. It was clear to me that this Fool guy really seemed to be the complete anarchist type.

Throm, in telling me more about the Fool's setup in Miami, pointed out a possible tactical error on the Fool's part. From what I learned, The Fool left his flank towards the zombie area unguarded because he figured that no one would ever get through those monsters. I gathered that if someone were able to get past the

22

zombies, there would be no guards because they think they are safe with this natural protection. This was definitely something I filed away for potential future use.

As we hoofed it back to Leadhead's crazy hover bike at the river, I stopped to grab the battery I had earlier stashed in the bushes outside of camp. Then Leadhead and I headed back to Jessica's aid, while I was hoping we weren't too late.

*****

As we hid Leadhead's bike near the subdivision, I was getting this paranoid feeling that Leadhead was planning to off me and take the girl to get the full bounty for himself. I liked the guy and he'd been pretty straight with me, but this was a very dog-eat-dog world and it wouldn't surprise me to see people double crossing each like that all the time.

We found Jack's boat that Jack and I stashed several days earlier and Leadhead and I took it across the river toward the zombie subdivision in Hollywood. As we climbed the embankment to make our way to the building, we were immediately attacked by three of those undead creatures.

Since it was daylight now, I had a much better look at them, but that was only more frightening.

It was a pretty fierce fight. They did take care of one problem for me--they killed Leadhead, which didn't overly concern me. I was also able to figure out some effective tactics against these slow-moving and slow-witted creatures and I quickly dispatched the three initial ones that attacked us plus a fourth that entered the fray late.

I grabbed up the heavy battery and dashed across the open field and into the building where the stasis pod was. Two more of those monstrous zombies emerged slowly from neighboring homes to attack me, but I dropped quickly into the pod and away from them. They apparently were too stupid to climb down the ladder, but I was concerned one might simply fall down into the pod. Nonetheless, they didn't come down after me.

It was pitch black down there in the pod and my heart sunk thinking I was too late. In the complete darkness, I found the place where the backup battery went and, as quickly as possible, I got the power back up and working.

Standing there bathed in the artificial light, I stared at Jessica's empty cryogenics tube. Somehow either she got out on her own or someone had already been there.

I started to climb back out of the pod and was fully expecting another nasty fight with the zombies that chased me into this hole. When I climbed near the top hatch, I heard Jessica and some guy arguing. Without a thought, I boldly burst up out of the hole to save her and I was confronted by four men who had very large rows of sharp teeth.

The look they gave me was extremely unsettling. These four brutes obviously had no problems with the undead and I was thinking they would probably kill Jessica and myself if I did anything, so I figured surrendering to them would buy us both some more time.

As they took my weapons, I found out these men--if I could call them that--worked for the same monster that Jack worked for. When they figured out who I was, one of them hit me in the head from behind and the lights went out.

As my mind fogged over into unconsciousness, I was hoping for the best, but I think I was more concerned for Mrs. Westgate than myself.

3

DIMENSION DEMONS

I am an American, fighting in the forces, which guard my country and our way of life. I am prepared to give my life in their defense. I will never forget that I am an American, fighting for freedom, responsible for my actions, and dedicated to the principles, which made my country free. I will trust in my God and in the United States of America.

~ United States Military Code of Conduct

It was funny how little those words of the Code of Conduct meant to me when I was going through Marine training. I still remember the training instructors drilling those into our heads every day. I remember doing one push up for every word of the code. That was a lot of pushups.

In the past week, since I had arrived in the future, I hadn't done one push up or one sit up...I needed to develop a conditioning regimen so I could focus my mind better with all the turmoil around me.

I was still stunned at my situation and hoped I'd wake up from the awful dream. But I wasn't dreaming, except when I actually slept...it was my most recent dream that seemed to bother me most and make me not want to sleep ever again.

I saw Private Ruiz, Captain Landry, Jessica, Leadhead, Jack, and my parents all shuffling towards me; their flesh was rotted away and their eye sockets blazed red. They drooled a green acidic goo from their dead lips and jagged teeth as they repeated over and over, "You killed us Tony...you killed us."

I ran from them, trying to flee, but they kept following me...the dream never ending. I heard Jack Luster's odd accent saying, "They never quit...they never sleep...they follow you forever." I ran into my house in Aurora, through the house, up the stairs, and into my room.

I heard Leadhead's voice in my head telling me, "If they bite you, you become one of them." I felt safe in my room, but when I looked in the mirror I saw myself all dead and withered--this thing of death--I had turned into a zombie myself.

It was then that I awoke…drenched in sweat, more due to the dream than the oppressive heat.

As if I was still living in a dream, my actual reality was probably more crazy. I found myself on a pedestal barely large enough for me to lay on, which sat in the center of a deep pit.

The stone and mortar room I was in appeared to be in a large, nondescript building. Although I was on this pedestal in the center of a pit, it was level with the floor of the rest of the room. Across the pit, standing very still in the room, was this fake skeleton with glowing red eyes. It was kind of a cool Halloween decoration, but really scary looking. The skeleton was holding a large axe and a big iron shield. It seemed like it was put there just to stare at me. They must have thought this would scare me, but it wasn't even very real looking.

What was real looking; however, was what was shambling around in the pit below me…it was Leadhead's zombified corpse!

It was then that my nightmare came rushing back at me in vivid colors. At that point I would say I was pretty scared.

After a few minutes of composing myself, I decided to stand up and take stock of my situation…that was when the skeleton moved and I was like, "Holy shit, it is real!" The skeleton seemed drawn to my actions…if I took a combative stance, it did as well.

After messing with the skeleton for a minute or so, I realized it couldn't reach me across the pit. So, I started checking other things out in regards to my predicament.

Whoever had brought me to this building left me without any weapons. With little to work with, I was able to pry a fist-sized rock loose from the pedestal I was on, so I tried to make a flail using the rock and my belt. I also still had my first aid kit, so I tried to add a sling from it to my contraption. I was testing it out when I dropped the whole damn thing into the pit with Leadhead.

I had a second sling in the kit, so I started working again, to make a smaller and less sturdy flail. This one actually worked, but it wasn't as impressive of a weapon as I had hoped.

Paying apt attention to the silent skeleton and the shambling zombie, I was able to pry up three more rocks. I put everything in my pockets, knowing I would probably need them later.

That was when I decided to take full stock of my situation. I measured out my wall-less prison--I was on a pedestal that was about five meters in diameter and about five meters up from the bottom of the pit that surrounded me. The edge of the pedestal was about seven meters from the outer edge of the pit, where the skeleton had moved to watch me closer.

I figured someone would be around soon to check on me, so I decided to get some more sleep while I waited.

"I will never surrender of my own free will. If in command, I will never surrender the members of my command while they still have the means to resist. If I am captured, I will continue to resist by all means available. I will make every effort to escape and aid others to escape. I will accept neither parole nor special favors from the enemy. If I become a prisoner of war, I will keep faith with my fellow prisoners. I will give no information or take part in any action, which might be harmful to my comrades. If I am senior, I will take command. If not, I will obey the lawful orders of those appointed over me and will back them up in every way. When questioned, should I become a prisoner of war, I am required to give name, rank, service number, and date of birth. I will evade answering further questions to the utmost of my ability. I will make no oral or written statements disloyal to my country and its allies or harmful to their cause."

So, there I was...it was dark in my mind and all I could think about at the time was that damn Military Code of Conduct.

I had already failed at the first code, "I will never surrender of my own free will." I actually gave up to those men, or those things with the pointed teeth. Thinking back, I'm not sure I had much of a choice. I wondered what would have happened to Mrs. Westgate if I had chosen to fight...would they have killed her? Of course I didn't know what actually did happen to her.

I couldn't seem to get Jessica out of my head...damn the Corps for sending me on that assignment in New York City. I almost wished at that point that I had died 150 years ago with everyone else.

I remembered, while I laid there on the stone pedestal, that both Jack and Leadhead had said something about a "Great Destruction." That was making me think about what had actually happened. I remembered the sirens and the public broadcasts. There were so many questions running around my head just then; "Was it a nuclear war or some kind of alien attack? I remembered that we had just sent our first starship into deep space. That made me wonder if our spaceship had come in contact with something or someone and it came here to destroy us. I didn't know if it was something like that or something entirely different.

Lying there on the cold stone, my head ached. I was thinking more about the code and how you were only to provide your name, rank, service number, and date of birth. That almost made me laugh aloud...my date of birth...I was thinking, "God, I'm 180 years old!"

Yes, it was clear that I needed to develop a regimen of fitness to focus my wandering mind.

I remembered Throm saying something about dragons to the west, living in the swamps...some place like Avalon or something. I remembered that he gave me a hand drawn map and I pulled it out and was looking it over. The name he used, "Dragons," was really odd. I was thinking they must be some kind of military group. That was when I thought maybe it was what was left of the U.S. Military since the "Great Destruction."

I determined that I still had many questions, but I had to make sure I didn't appear too dumb about the new world I was in. It was very clear that I couldn't let everyone know I was a sleeper--that would be too dangerous.

When I finally slept enough and was bored enough, I actually felt pretty refreshed. From some light filtering in through the roof of the building, I could tell it was probably the next morning, but it was possible I slept for longer. That damn skeleton was still just standing there staring at me.

I awoke pretty hungry and was glad that I picked up some dried fruit at the outpost. Since no one had showed up that I was aware of, I decided to start yelling to get someone's attention. Unfortunately, no one ever came.

That was when I started to think that they just left me there to rot. I decided it was time to take matters into my own hands.

I looked down into the pit, really giving it a good examination. There was a metal ladder attached to the wall leading down from the pedestal into the pit and one on the other side leading up out of the pit. Both of the ladders were affixed to the wall. Leadhead still had his leather armor, revolver, and a nice-looking fire axe on his back, but being a zombie I doubted he would use the weapons against me.

I decided it would be best to kill Leadhead--again--before I did anything.

I pulled the three rocks out of my pocket, and tested their weight. I took aim straight at Leadhead's head and blasted him three times in rapid succession. It was just like being at a fair and trying to knock over milk bottles with a softball.

After the third rock sailed into his cranium, he fell, twitching on the floor.

I dropped down, gathered up my rocks, took his revolver and axe, and then cut his head off--that stopped the twitching. Chopping his head off made me wonder if zombies stayed dead or if they could come back to life again and again.

After I searched the rest of Leadhead, I took his thick leather armor jacket and boots and found some matches and cigarettes he had on him. I also picked up my belt and stashed the sling I had tied to it back with my first aid supplies.

That was when I turned my attention to the skeleton. It was leaning over the edge of the pit with its empty sockets staring down at me. After some careful consideration, I decided it was simply best to climb up and fight the damn thing with my newly acquired axe.

I climbed up the ladder and accepted a quick hit against my now leathered back as I cleared the edge of the pit. I scrambled to engage the skeletal nightmare and we went to blows.

Here I was thinking that because it was only made of bones that it would be pretty weak and easy to destroy, but man I was wrong. Not only was it as quick as me, but it was better than the fighting simulators I used in training. I had my ass handed to me by a damn skeleton!

Finally I got away from the horror show by dropping back down into the pit. Bleeding and bruises, I climbed back up on the pedestal and collapsed in pain and disgust.

I think I simply passed out, but after sleeping I felt a bit better. The good thing was that I didn't remember my dreams that time.

When I woke back up, there it was, across the pit, grinning at me with its glowing red eyes. Well, grinning may be an exaggeration, but it was still very unnerving.

I decided to take a different approach with the skeleton than the head-to-head failure from earlier. I decided to try to take the monster out with my throwing rocks like I did with Leadhead. After throwing all the rocks I had, it was clear my throwing arm wasn't major league material. It was a lot easier to hit Leadhead because he moved so slow and never blocked anything thrown at him.

Throwing caution to the wind, I leveled off with Leadhead's revolver and pumped four rounds into the skeleton.

The first shot slammed into the skeleton's skull really hurting it, but it was able to get its shield in the way of the next two shots. The last shot was low--too low for it to block. That bullet killed it by ripping through the bones of its foot.

Out of ammo again, I climbed down into the pit and back out of the pit. The Halloween decoration was nothing but a pile of bones, so I added its shield to my inventory. The skeleton's axe wasn't quite as nice as the axe I took from Leadhead, but it was so heavy that I needed two hands to use it. That made me think, because I remember that the skeleton was only using it one-handed and had his shield in his other hand.

The weirdest thing I found when searching the pile of bones was a key inside the skeleton's head. I considered how oddly strange that was as I took it.

There was a small hall near the end of the big stone room and a door by that hall leading out of the building. First, I checked out the hall and at the end of it there was a small crack in the wall. I heard some odd buzzing sounds behind it. I checked it for some kind of electrical trap and although I didn't find anything, I still wasn't too sure.

I went back to the door out of the room and found it locked; yet the key that I found in the skeleton's head unlocked it.

Since there was nothing else in the room I was in and no other way out, I decided to check out the only exit. Listening at the closed door, I could hear the buzzing sound in the room, but it was much more faint than by the crack down the hall.

I cracked the door open to get a look inside and I heard the buzzing sound speed for the door. Before I could get a look in the room beyond, I shut the door as something slammed into it on the other side.

I went back down the hall to the crack in the wall and whatever was buzzing around in the other room, followed me back to that crack. When I returned back to the door, the buzzing didn't follow me, so I quickly opened the door and looked in.

Inside the room, I saw three huge, dog-sized mosquitoes with spear-like stingers. There were two glowing metal pots on stands that provided light in the room. I could make out, across the room, a person lying still on the floor and holding some type of gun in its hand.

I also could see another door out of the adjacent room, but it was closed. In my quick review of the room, it appeared as if the huge mosquitoes had killed the person lying in the corner. Of course, the flying bugs immediately advanced at me when I opened the door, so I closed it fast.

This time, I went back by the crack and tried to look through it, but the bugs kept trying to attack me even though they couldn't get their big stingers through the crack. I was going to use my newly acquired revolver on them, but I remembered that I was out of ammo.

Considering my options, I finally determined my best bet was to charge across the room, grab the weapon from the dead body, and charge back. If it really was a gun, I thought I might possibly shoot those things through the crack, but if I fought all three at once in the room, they would probably kill me.

Since I was still pretty beat up from the fight with the skeleton, I decided to rest as much as possible to heal my earlier injuries.

After a long quiet sleep, I put my plan in motion. After having serious trouble dodging the giant stingers and some poor luck, I finally got the gun-like thing off the body and stumbled back through the door, much worse for the wear. When I examined the weapon, it turned out to be a big bug sprayer of all things. I simply figured that it had to have some effect on these bugs, but I wasn't sure what.

Going back down the hall, I took aim through the crack and blasted one of the mosquitoes that was frantically trying to attack me. Whatever was in the gas canisters was obviously a strong poison to them as the mosquito seemed really hurt by the spray. The problem was it was still alive and it looked like there was only enough propellant for three more shots.

The second shot killed the mosquito I hurt initially and another one quickly took its place at the crack in the wall. These were very fanatic, but also really stupid creatures. I squirted that one with a blast of the sprayer, but it seemed much more resilient to the poison and shook off the blast, which wasn't good at all. I blasted it again and the spray barely hurt it.

Out of liquid in the canister and not having many other choices, I decided to charge back out there in the room in hopes that the body might have more spray canisters to load in the sprayer. My luck definitely improved this time and I made it to the body without getting hurt. On the dead person's belt I found two more canisters.

Grabbing one of the canisters and quickly loading it, I blocked the attacks of the mosquitoes with the skeleton's iron shield. As one of the mosquitoes buzzed in to attack me, I gave it a solid shot in the face with the newly reloaded sprayer. It wasn't the one I hurt earlier, but it died immediately.

The last one jabbed its enormous stinger at me again just as I sprayed it. As I engulfed it in a cloud of gas, its stinger slammed into my chest. I watched the mosquito crumple to the floor as everything went black.

*****

I awoke again in complete pain, which had become a very common feeling those days. When my vision cleared, I found myself tied to a chair and staring straight into the face of that wicked being that was Jack Luster's old boss.

It was just then that I remembered the name Jack called him; "Veto Slako."

Immediately he started talking to me--ranting actually--and I immediately recognized him, but that couldn't have been possible. I knew this guy. He was the black guy I pushed in front of 150 years ago at the transporter station in New York City!

He was going on and on about being trapped in some "demon dimension" for 150 years because of me and unless I could give him a really good reason, he was going to kill me.

My head was spinning with pain and all I could think of was to be a Marine hard ass with my immediate responses. Being tied to a chair makes it hard to get up in someone's grill, but I gave it my best shot. This; however, just made him even angrier at me and suddenly I was overcome with this almost uncontrollable feeling of fear.

At this point, I was so pissed off and depressed over my whole situation, I was just itching for him to end the nightmare and kill me.

Goading him to end it all, he grinned wickedly and said he not only would kill me, but then he would have his way with the woman I was with. That was when I realized that he had Jessica!

I snapped back to reality and devised a quick plan to save myself.

With my fair share of anger, I was able to muster enough courage to rationalize his current situation to him. I told him that 150 years ago, I cut in front of him to use the transporter. Thus, he stepped in right after me, but just as he did, the Great Destruction, whatever it was, occurred and the transporter trapped him for 150 years in the transporter dimension--what he called the demon dimension. For those 150 years, he seethed and stewed, focusing totally on hating me for trapping him, but he never realized that if he had actually made it to Queens, New York, which was his final destination, he would have been dead in the Great Destruction like everyone else.

My rationalization seemed to make him stop and think and, looking a bit befuddled, he stormed out of the room to think about what I said, leaving me with only the instructions of not to try to escape.

I was able to get untied and finally able to get a good look around at the chamber I was in. I found Jessica sleeping in a huge birdcage suspended from the ceiling in one of the corners of the room. I woke her and tried to pick the lock, but all my attempts failed, which made it clear to me that I wouldn't make it as a professional thief.

Distraught and still in the cage, Jessica told me her story.

She used to be a low-level ad exec, which confirmed my sense that she wasn't anyone important in Heliogistics. She told me she was, or is, married to this guy named Bradley. Bradley, turned out to be a big wig in Heliogistics and they had been married for about a year when Yellow Mike hit the scene. Jessica, thinking to the future, invested in a plan to put both of them in stasis, but Bradley had friends working on a cure and he was getting a bit weird on her. Because he was acting so strange, she left their home in Michigan and went to Heliogistics headquarters. There she barricaded herself in her office, unsure about what to do.

She continued her story. On 14 Aug 2045, Jessica received a call from some purchasing agent in Heliogistics named Monica Herkamur who said she had a big surprise for her and Bradley and she should come to Monica's home. Jessica called Bradley and he corroborated the story so she went to Monica's mansion and no one appeared to be around. However, she heard piano music upstairs, which caused her to investigate. When she went upstairs she found Bradley and Monica bumping uglies on the carpet.

Jessica said that when they turned to her, they both had pointed teeth, like dog's teeth or fangs and they said something about finding a cure for the Yellow Mike.

She fled Monica's house in horror and hatred even as they yelled at her to come back. She returned to her office at Heliogistics and was contemplating either using the cryogenics pod, or offing herself when I called from downstairs.

Of course she believed I was working for Bradley and trying to bring her back. I agreed with her that, if her husband was such a high-roller in Heliogistics he probably organized the mission I was on, since I hadn't really figured out what the Marines would want with an advertising executive. However, I ensured her that I had no idea what was going on, or if he was behind it...I was just following orders.

Sitting there alone in Veto's chamber, we compared some notes and she told me, she actually found out the current date was 2196. That would mean we were actually asleep for 151 years. She also believed the Great Destruction was indeed a nuclear war from what she had learned.

After hearing everything she had learned, I gave her some basic information that I had found out and told her what I knew about Veto Slako. She was really worried about Veto, especially when we discussed what might have happened to his mind while he was trapped for 150 years. Jessica told me about tests that ran on animals and that if they left one in the transporter dimension, even for a very short amount of time, it would exhibit serious mental problems. That was when I actually realized then that his hatred of me trapping him in the demon dimension might actually have saved him from going totally insane.

Not being able to pick the lock on the cage, I tried to break Jessica out with my axe, but that didn't work. Just as I was pounding away at the lock, Veto came back in the room--he probably heard me bashing on the cage.

He was a bit pissed that I was trying to get Jessica out of the cell, but he had decided that I was right and that he would be dead now if it wasn't for me.

I decided to reinforce his opinion of me and led him through an explanation of past experiments with dimensional transporters on animals and how they would suffer serious mental problems after only an hour or so in his demon dimension. I explained to him, that his focused hatred of me probably saved his mind, as it were, while the fact that I cut in line saved his life.

My attempt to curry more favor with him seemed to work and, although he didn't appear to like it, he realized I was kind of right. Veto grudgingly released

Jessica from the cage and I had to help her out due to her legs falling fast asleep. Holding her against me, I was pleasantly surprised that she still smelled really nice even after 151 years.

Veto asked me where I wanted to go.

I asked him if he could get us to Homestead. I wasn't sure how he was going to get us there, but that was where I thought was best for us to go at the time.

He seemed a bit surprised that we would want to go to Homestead, but I explained it away and he waved a hand in front of us.

4

HOMESTEAD

I remember an excerpt of something from a historical study I did on Native Americans serving in the military. "The requirements for successful military service -- strength, bravery, pride, and wisdom - match those of the Indian warrior. Military service affords an outlet for combat that fulfills a culturally-determined role for the warrior. Therefore, the military is an opportunity for cultural self-fulfillment. By sending young tribal members off to be warriors, they return with experiences that make them valued members of their society. Additionally, the military provides educational opportunities, which allow Native American veterans to return to their community with productive job skills to improve their quality of life."

~ Tony Moon

The next thing I knew, Jessica and I were standing in the middle of what was left of Homestead Air Force Base in Florida.

Pretty quickly, we were challenged by a guard who was manning an impressive pulse cannon on one of the walls surrounding the base. We explained the basics around our situation and finally we convinced him to allow us that to enter Homestead.

He told us that we had to shed everything but our undergarments in order to be scanned for traces of Yellow Mike. I assumed this was to prove we were sleepers.

I was a bit concerned about Jessica stripping to her undies, but she didn't seem overly concerned and disrobed right there. I tried not to look, but really couldn't help it--what a body!

After we dropped everything, one of the storage shelters, across the flightline, slowly opened up and he motioned for us to go in. Inside there was a polished set of steel stairs leading down underground. We headed downstairs, just as he called out from behind us, "Welcome to Homestead."

With that, the doors closed behind us and I immediately felt a bit safer somehow.

As we went down the long flight of metal stairs, many things were going through my mind.

Veto may have been a really scary thing, but I was thinking that he might prove to be more an ally to us now than an enemy. I thought back to him calling his confinement as the "Demon Dimension" and that gave me the chills. It was almost as if he was saying that Dimensional Transportation opened up some type of portal to a demon world, or maybe that was just how it seemed to him being trapped in there for 150 years. Judging by Veto's odd burnt and angular appearance, I wondered if Veto had actually become some kind of demon. He certainly looked like something one might attribute to a demon. I also was wondering if the four who knocked me out in Hollywood were also lesser demons. The more I thought about it, the more terrified I became of the concept--maybe that would explain my irrational feeling of fear around them.

Jessica's story also disturbed me quite a bit. First, I found that I was really beginning to like her; probably more physically than emotionally right now, but I felt like I got her into this and I should be the one to protect her. Now I found out that she was, or is, married to someone with fangs, who was caught sleeping with another woman. The whole statement about Bradley and Monica finding a cure for the Yellow Mike and them having fangs like a dog made my skin tingle. I knew my thoughts were a little silly, but if we opened a door to a demon world and zombies, skeletons, and magic exist in the world today, I was supposing on the possibility that Monica's gift was one of immortality--as in vampirism.

Descending the stairs in the fluorescent-lit staircase really made it seem ludicrous, but nothing at that point seemed too far-fetched to me. Regardless, based off what little I knew about the world of necromancy, a vampire probably wouldn't be affected by Yellow Mike.

My major concern, if this were true though, was that would mean that Bradley and Monica could still be alive, or living dead as it were, since vampires were immortal. Since they were in Michigan last, they could have been far enough away from any blast zones in the nuclear war that would have killed them. I also believed that anything like a vampire might be very strong, so they probably could have survived the attack and existed all these years.

Of course, at this point, I was just imagining these things...that would be like me thinking that Throm was actually talking about scaly, flying dragons, when he was talking about that place to the west, and not some group, or army. I was just letting my imagination get away from me now that we were pretty safe.

Thinking back to Veto though...he said he had been trapped for 150 years. That caused me to think about how and exactly when did he get out of the dimension. I was kicking myself for not asking him when I had the chance. It seemed a rather odd coincidence that he would be trapped as long as we were asleep--like our fates were somehow linked.

Considering Veto and everything that happened, that triggered other memories about who those four men at Heliogistics were. I was still wondering if they were responsible for the explosion and if not, what would have caused it to happen. That was an odd turn of events that didn't seem to make sense--was it just another coincidence?

Getting to the bottom of the long well-lit set of stairs, I considered; Dimensional Power could have been feeding off a demon dimension as well. It might be no wonder everyone was getting infected with Yellow Mike, which was a disease that made people insane, like what happened to the animals left too long in the demon dimension. I was thinking that our own power and transportation systems could have been leaking this dimension right into our world and our minds.

*****

After my father retired from the Air Force, he took up a job as a Private Pilot Instructor. He would always open his training of new pilots with his favorite quote about luck versus skill. He believed there were too many pilots out there flying by the seat of their pants and relying on luck versus learning to become really good pilots. I never really understood what he meant until now. In the last month, or so, I had gotten by pretty much on luck and very little on my actual skills. Although, and my father would probably agree, luck can be very crucial, it wasn't going to save me every time...it would be skill that would make the difference! Thanks Dad.

> *"Those who rely on luck, die without skill."*
> *-- Lt Col (Ret) Brian Moon*

Jessica and I entered Homestead through a large door at the bottom of the stairs. The door opened on its own into a very large airlock that several people could fit into. We stepped in and the door shut behind us.

A voice emitted from a hidden speaker requested Jessica's name, which she gave. The voice instructed her to move through the next door out of the room. I squeezed her hand and reassured her that everything would be all right, which I hoped to be true. That reminded me of a commercial on television about deodorant where they used to say, "Never let 'em see you sweat!"

After a couple minutes or so, which I wasn't sure of because my watch was left upstairs, the voice returned asking me to identify myself. With military precision, I provided my name, rank, service number, and date of birth. I was directed to step into the next room, which I did. This was a smaller airlock, which looked like it was designed for about one person. After the door whooshed shut, a visible gas hissed into the room.

I calmed myself and controlled my breathing hoping that this was just part of some "scanning mechanism" and sure enough, I saw some laser beams in the gas reading my body's exterior makeup. I was pretty sure at this point that it was a way for Homestead to keep pollutants, like Yellow Mike, out of the shelter we were about to enter.

When the other door opened, I was greeted by a man in a gray uniform standing in a very high-tech looking metal hallway and carrying an assault rifle. The man wore a nametape on his uniform identifying him as "Crash" and I immediately noted he wore the U.S. Army rank of Sergeant, so I greeted him as "Sergeant Crash."

He led me to a lounge across the hall, where Jessica was waiting. She was now wearing a white robe and Sergeant Crash handed me one as well. Jessica asked me what this place was and I gave her a quick rundown about what I knew about Homestead. I think it was enough at the time to calm her fears.

Just then, a redheaded woman in a similar gray uniform entered from another doorway. She was wearing a lab coat over her uniform and had silver bars on her collars denoting her as a Navy Lieutenant or captain in any other service. She was slightly attractive, but had this definite air about her as being really intelligent...kind of librarian-like.

The new woman introduced herself as Captain Lisa Scott. Captain Scott asked me to join her in the other room so she could ask me some questions. Again I ensured Jessica that everything would fine.

The room we entered was small and looked like an interrogation or interviewing room. That immediately put me on the defensive, but it was obvious that the captain tried to remove any physical barriers by sitting down near me, versus across the table from me. This told me she was either very skilled at interrogation, she was some kind of shrink, or she just didn't know any better. At least she trusted me enough to get that close. I was sizing her up and she seemed kind of weak; so much so that I suspected that one good hit would probably knock her out. Of course I misread the skeleton earlier and figured it was best to not find out.

She started to ask me about myself and I provided her with my basic military responses, which were name, rank, service number, and date of birth. She asked me if I was hungry or need anything, but refusing to accept any favors at this point, I simply stated, "No," although I was actually starving.

Then I decided to apply some of my counter-interrogation training and turned the tables on her by asking her some pointed questions. She openly shared with me that she was an Air Force Captain and told me that survivors from before the Great Destruction can keep their rank titles at Homestead, if they want. This answer led me to believe she was a sleeper versus a sheltie, but I didn't ask. She went on to tell me I could still be considered a Lance Corporal here unless I chose to adopt the appropriate Air Force rank, which was Airmen First Class. I told her that I'd like to remain a Lance Corporal if that was all right with them.

Based on our conversation, I was feeling much more confident that she wasn't a threat and decided to give her a quick synopsis of the events that led to us arriving at Homestead.

Captain Scott asked some rather mundane questions like when I enlisted and when I entered the sleeper pod. She seemed to be a bit surprised when she found out Jessica and I barely escaped the Great Destruction.

After talking for a little while, she realized how horribly injured I was. I guess I was doing a pretty good job of covering things like that up.

She provided me two Stichpacks, which I fondly remember from training. We used to call it "Slamming Down" in the Marines. We would be issued them after brutal physical training. Some Marines got rather addicted to them in Recon Training due to excessive use and washed out. I tried not to use them as much as the other guys, so I didn't develop any specific tendencies towards them. Now; however, I used the two, applying them in the "textbook manner" and felt right as rain a second later.

After I cleared my head of pain, I remembered the lady I left in the sleeper pod by Regan's outpost. I immediately informed the captain, which gave her a bit of concern. She explained that sleeper pods were supposed to open based on a signal sent from Cold Stasis Technologies, but something went wrong and the signals were never sent. There was a failsafe built into the pods so that if the generator failed, the backup battery would perform an emergency revival of anyone in stasis.

It turned out that the generators had an approximate 150-year lifespan and over the past couple of years Sleepers had started just waking up like we did.

She pulled out a Soul Man, a minicomputer normally kept strapped to one's forearm, and I showed her, on a rough-drawn map, where the pod was located. Noticing the rough drawing on the Soul Man screen, I asked why it wasn't a satellite-generated map and she told me there were no satellites anymore due to decaying orbits. I should have asked about the inertial positioning technology we used 150 years ago, but forgot.

I also found out that this underground compound was originally built by the Air Force to store nuclear weapons--probably a weapon storage and security system (WS3) area. I remembered reading about those nuclear storage systems in a history book. Long after the base was closed, Cold Stasis Technology bought it out and refurbished it to be a massive shelter. They sold rooms and bunks to those interested for large sums of money. The residents of this shelter started emerging about 120 years after the Great Destruction.

The captain told me the Great Destruction was actually a fully automated nuclear war and no one knew who or what actually started it. I figured they hadn't considered the possible reasons for Yellow Mike, as I had, because they were still using Dimensional Power in the shelter. I didn't ask it, but wondered if there were any transporters known to still be active.

I asked the captain if anyone had thought about trying to find a Cold Stasis Technology Control Center in the hope of discovering where all the sleepers were and start reviving them before they were revived like we were--on our own. She hadn't heard anything about this, but took note of the idea. She told me that Cold

Stasis Technology was decentralized, so there could be several possible control centers across the country and it might be a good idea.

Even though I had numerous other questions, she asked if I would undergo another test--military related-- and I accepted...they did, after all, give me two Stichpacks. I left the room and told Jessica that the captain wanted to ask her some questions and not to be afraid. As convincingly as possible, I told her we'd see each other later.

Sergeant Crash escorted me to another room down the hall and it was a simulator, similar to the ones I used in Marine training. He programmed the sim for a desert landscape with a cave entrance and created a powerful revolver for me to use and simple gray uniform for me to wear. The basic rules of engagement were for me to go into the cave and bring back a blue orb. This was a pretty standard "capture the flag" training-type sim that I had seen many times.

I walked into the cave carefully, knowing my moves were probably being monitored by Crash or some technician. They used these sims to teach as well as evaluate and I was pretty used to having a lot of crazy things thrown at me during a sim session.

The first thing I encountered was this grotesque green humanoid with horns and sharp fangs. He was armed with an interesting club and some throwing weapons. The creature spoke to me in garbled English, calling himself, "Goblin Dork."

Two shots later from my explosive revolver and Goblin Dork was nothing but a piece of nasty green Swiss cheese on the tunnel floor. Realizing that I only had four shots left and how crucial ammo tended to be, I scrounged the dead body for anything that would help going forward. I took his fancy club and the throwing knives. They were meager items, but you never know what might come in handy in a training simulation.

I pushed through some thick vines to meet the next holographic entity in my little test. The reality of the simulations these machines create always amazed me and were hard to get used to.

Just beyond the heavy vines, I encountered a larger version of Goblin Dork, who, when he spoke, sounded about as dumb as the last computer generation. This one announced himself as, "Goblin Lackey." Not only bigger, he was a bit better armed to boot--not a surprise, since these test your abilities on an escalating scale. Lackey turned out to definitely be a bit more difficult, but I used my Marine training to get in a good fighting position and I put two out of my three shots into him before I finished him off with Goblin Dork's club.

I exchanged the club for Lackey's heavy sword, a wooden shield, and a couple pieces of leather armor, which fit relatively well. Newly outfitted with sim-constructed weapons and armor, I moved on. I was a bit beat down, but I knew that when the simulation finished, the simulation-generated pain would go away, so I pressed on. I figured it would be good to put on a show for Homestead and not disappoint the ones watching my progress.

There was another vine barrier that I had to push through to get to the biggest green creature so far. As a matter of fact, he was holding a sword I don't think I could have even swung! The monster was wearing full leather armor and carrying a huge steel shield. Seeing this massive monster tower over me with that sword in one hand and shield in the other, I started thinking that the blue orb I was supposed to retrieve was a lot further away than I initially thought.

I tried to intimidate the brute with some vicious boasts of my skills against the previous two encounters, but I certainly wasn't as effective as I would have liked. Without a similar introduction as the others, this beast waded in for his attack and I spent my last precious round hoping to blow a nice hole between his evil red-rimmed eyes.

No luck. My arm got mired in the heavy draping vines and it threw off my shot. This brute was on me like an animal in no time and I tried desperately to block his crushing attacks. The first solid blow literally shattered my puny wooden shield to pieces. With what remained of the shield, I was able to block his second and third attack, but I couldn't get my tangled arm free of the stupid vines. That was when the fourth swing blasted through my shield and armor, crushing into me.

Just as the massive sword hit me, the simulation ended and a warning sound started screeching over the speaker system about some biohazard leak in the compound. My injuries--of course--vanished as did all the weapons I was carrying. I was back to my white robe, t-shirt, and boxers...formidable, I know.

I finally got the simulator's entrance to open and stepped out just when Sergeant Crash came running by. The sergeant yelled to me to sit and wait while he went through a door at the end of the hall. I was really getting sick of being told to wait around, so I decided to go and check on Jessica and the captain.

Jessica wasn't in the waiting room, but the captain was. She informed me that there had been some type of containment leak in the lab down the hall. She directed me to go help Sergeant Crash, which was against his order to wait, but she outranked him. I was just glad to be doing something instead of sitting around. Before I headed back to the door Crash went through, the captain gave me her pistol, which was pretty insignificant compared to the simulated revolver I had been wielding a few minutes ago.

I stepped back out into the hall and started towards the other door when Sergeant Crash entered the hall without his weapon in hand. He started shambling towards me in a very familiar way--all too familiar way as of late. I realized from the vacant expression on his face and displayed mannerisms that I would now need to refer to him as Sergeant "Zombie" Crash.

Fighting the mounting fear inside me, I put a single bullet in his head. I thought, as his blood splattered on the nice clean walls, "God I hope I'm right and he's now a zombie." It was obvious, from the way his head split apart, that he had been a zombie, because he continued to move toward me. Just as he reached me, I pressed the muzzle of the pistol against his cranium and pulled the trigger. The noncommissioned officer's head exploded and he dropped to the ground wriggling about.

I called the captain and she freaked out when she saw Crash writhing on the floor. I calmed her down and then used a chair to bash the rest of Crash's head in until he stopped moving. I didn't see any reason to waste precious ammo.

Captain Scott told me the leak must have been the "Zombie Gas" they had been experimenting with. She told me that the leak would have to be stopped in the lab, or the rest of the shelter would be lost.

I grabbed a really nice knife off Crash's dead body and we used Captain Scott's communicator to contact the control center in the shelter. The control center advised us that we needed to seal the leak in the lab immediately. They estimated at least four scientists were in the lab at the time of the accident. I informed the captain that I would try to seal the leak, but I asked her to get Jessica and be ready to head up to the surface if I failed. After all, they had that cannon upstairs on the perimeter wall and if zombies started pouring out of Homestead, it could vaporize them.

The captain figured going into the lab was suicide, but I told her I saw no other way. Before I went through the door to the lab, I had the control center explain to me what the lab looked like, where I would find the leak, and how I should go about shutting it off. They also shared with me where the chemical protective gear was in the lab if I could make it that far. From their information, I expected a hall on the other side of the door and a closed-off lab to the right. They also told me there would be a window in the hall that looked into the lab.

I was hoping the hall would be empty, but when I opened the door, there were two zombies shambling about in a green gas-filled corridor. There appeared to be a crack in the lab's observation window and the gas had filled the corridor. The zombies alerted on my Marine ass and started toward me immediately. It was interesting to notice how they alerted to me, even though I hadn't made a sound. It was almost as it they sensed or smelled me, which made me wonder if there was a way to throw zombies off the scent.

I stepped back into the clear air of the hallway and waited for them to come to me. I didn't see much sense breathing in that gas if I didn't have to. The two shambled through and, after a couple ineffective semi-automatic blasts with the captain's pistol, they cornered me at the other end of the hall. At first they got their vice-like hands on me, but miraculously I slipped out of their grasp, got past them, and charged down the hall.

As I passed the door to the simulator, I considered trying to go back inside and use the system against the zombified lab techs, but I remembered that the system shut down when the leak occurred and the simulator probably wouldn't have been working at that point. The thought crossed my mind as to if they even would recognize the computer generated simulation at all in their vegetated undead state.

As I passed the simulator door, I remembered that Sergeant Crash was carrying an assault rifle when he went into the other hall. I thought I remembered seeing it on the floor of the hall and added some urgency to my run.

I charged the rest of the way down the hall and through the door and there the rifle sat, under the cracked lab window. Holding my breath, I sprinted to the rifle and could hear more zombies shuffling around in the lab. Ignoring the threat in the lab, I scooped up the assault rifle and spun on the two zombies scuffling after me.

Just as I leveled the newly acquired weapon on the open doorway, I was hit by the initial effect of the Zombie Gas. Even though I was holding my breath, I could feel it tearing at my whole body and wracking me in pain. When the two zombies came through the open door, I opened up on them spraying the hallway with a full burst from the rifle. Even racked in pain, the explosive power of the weapon against a real enemy was exhilarating!

One of the living corpses dropped instantly under the barrage of automatic gunfire, however, he shielded some of the shots to the second, and it kept moving toward me. Just as I squeezed off a second, shorter burst from the rifle, another wave of pain coursed through my veins and threw off my aim. The damn zombie was still barely alive, but was able to grab me again and this time I was too weak to get away.

Just as this horrid thing took a killing-bite out of my exposed scalp, the walls of the simulator appeared and everything else vanished. That's when I realized that I had been duped by the reality of the machine's simulations.

Damn those simulators were realistic...I never realized I was still in the simulator that whole time.

It turned out, this was all a ruse to test my potential loyalty to the shelter and not only did I pass, but it appeared as if I impressed the hell out of the staff. I guess they figured anyone else would have bolted when the gas started eating at them, yet I stayed and fought to the death for the shelter, even when it looked pretty hopeless. It also seemed that they were pretty impressed that I did so well against the zombies. I think if the simulated gas wasn't eating away at me, I could have made it through alive.

When I looked back on the whole exercise, I wondered to myself, "Why would I die for people I didn't even know?" I figured that was just a byproduct of my Marine training and warrior spirit.

*****

After the simulation was over, Jessica and I were escorted further into the complex of Homestead. I wasn't surprised when the door at the end of the hall didn't actually lead to a lab, like it did in the simulation. As a matter of fact, it turned out to be a security checkpoint, pretty much like I should have expected to begin with.

They quickly processed us in and escorted us to some really luxurious guest quarters. Jessica had the room across the hall from me. They informed us that dinner would be in about two hours. All my gear was stored neatly in closets and drawers, except my silly impoverished flail, which was lying out on the bed.

When I said this place was luxurious, I meant like the Ritz!

Just as I was checking out the bathroom, I heard a buzz at my door. I was wondering who it could be and actually hoped it would be Jessica standing there when I opened the door, but instead it was Sergeant Crash.

Crash told me that he would come get us in two hours for dinner, but really wanted to straighten out a few details that Captain Scott had been confused about. Turned out, the ranks used at Homestead were Marine based, not whatever service you wanted as she had told me. Crash was wearing Army stripes because that was what they could get hold of and they were the same rank stripes as a Marine Sergeant's, which he was.

Crash also told me that my oath of enlistment held no weight in Homestead since I took it when there was an American President and things had changed, thus they changed the oath. Obviously they didn't want me going around thinking I was automatically part of their militaristic group just because I was a Marine 150 years ago.

I was a bit surprised that the captain had the rank structure wrong, which seemed like such a rudimentary thing, but I dismissed it when he told me she was just a medical officer. I figured I would ask her more about it again if I had the chance.

I asked him where he got the name Crash. Turns out his real name was Crishowski and Crash was just easier for everyone to say and spell, so he adopted that. In the Marines I grew up in, you would have your last name on your uniform regardless of how it was spelled and you'd like it, but obviously it wasn't as strict at Homestead.

Crishowski left and I decided it was time to peel the layers of grime from my body so I stripped and kicked on the shower as hot as it could go.

As I let the bathroom steam up, I took a little time to knock out 100 push-ups and 100 sit-ups. It really felt good to mentally and physically focus myself for a few minutes. As I walked into the steam-filled bathroom, I experienced a momentary flashback to the simulator where I was faced with two zombies in the gas-filled hallway. I quickly dismissed the similarity and plunged headfirst into the scalding hot water.

I was really looking forward to a hot shower and real meal. I survived off that dried fruit, but it was getting old fast. It seemed like forever since I'd even had a shower--well about 150 years actually!

I slowly pruned up in the stall as I took my time--
almost an hour--thoroughly enjoying the feeling of
being clean again. I'd trained in the field before for
days on end, but this was probably the best after-field
shower I had ever had!

As the hot water soothed away the past few weeks,
so many thoughts ran through my head. I was full of
questions and wanted to ask everything I could from
someone at that point, but I had no one to talk to. I
decided to log my questions away in order to ask them
the first chance I got.

I really thought I was on to something regarding
finding a Cold Stasis Technology Control Center and
finding a map of where all the other sleeper pods were,
what condition they were in, and who might be in
them. If I could find the closest control center,
Homestead could send out an expedition to it and I
wanted to be part of that.

I remembered that we sent a deep space ship into
space right before the Great Destruction. It was called
the *Bard Endeavor*. Being as it was now 150 years later,
I wondered if it had ever returned. Normally, it would
have landed at Cape Canaveral in Florida. Not being
familiar with the state, I had no idea how close we were
to the Cape, but that might be worth checking out or at
least asking about.

As the hot water cascaded off my face, I started
thinking about the Homestead shelter. I wondered if
there were other shelters like this one and, if so, where.

It would be very helpful to the residents of Homestead to have some allies in the war against the Fool.

Thinking about what was left after the Great Destruction, made me consider the full impact of the war. There had to be areas around the world that were not impacted by the nuclear war and remained untouched by the Great Destruction.

Thinking about my list of dwindling supplies and reminiscing on the feeling of the revolver and assault rifle made me think about my meager equipment issue. I was wondering how one would go about outfitting themselves in this new world. Would it be as I had been doing it--taking weapons off the dead and bartering one item for another? It was important to me to improve my ability to fight off these post-apocalyptic horrors and I was obviously going to need some better firepower to be successful.

The more I considered my situation, the more I thought about the war between Homestead and the Fool. Homestead obviously could use help in their fight with the Fool, but I wondered if any organized military was actually still around. I thought maybe the "Dragons" that Throm referred to might be able to help us—with a name like that, they had to be some powerful military-type organization or group.

Of course, thinking about the word dragons, brought other monstrous names to mind. Obviously, zombies and demons somehow existed as did some mystical power that sure looked like magic. That made me question if dragons were in fact just that--dragons of legend. Then I wondered if vampires, like in the movies and books, existed too. Obviously, I had found out the hard way that a person's body could remain "alive" as an undead zombie, so a vampire had to be possible.

Yellow Mike really seemed to have had a devastating effect on the planet--way beyond anything from 2045. I wondered if anyone in the past 150 years had figured out where Yellow Mike actually came from. Thinking about the simulation Homestead tricked me with, I really started to wonder if they were actually experimenting with some kind of zombie gas and if this gas was some kind of airborne Yellow Mike. It made me wonder if everyone that died in this world would come back to life as a zombie or if you had to die a certain way or in a certain place. I also wondered if the twitching zombies actually came back to life or if they would lay there and twitch forever...that sent a cold shudder up my spine as I stepped out of the shower.

I got slightly tangled in the shower curtain and had a flashback to the vines in the simulator. That huge green monster in the simulator reminded me a lot of Throm Burlash. The first two I fought referred to themselves as "Goblins." I wondered if Throm was actually considered a goblin as well and what other types of monsters from myth and folklore existed today.

As I toweled off in front of the bathroom mirror other things ran through my head. I still owed that kindly woman I called grandma the money for healing me. If the shelter had simulator technology they had to have the capability to provide training in important skills for the world today. I needed to find out what Homestead knew about Veto Slako and I still knew where we stashed Leadhead's hover bike. If hover bikes were still used, I suspected there had to be other forms of modern transportation, like cars and planes.

I stared into the mirror at a new scar forming on my face and wondered if any of the dimensional transporters were still active and even if I would be willing to test one.

I wrapped a towel around my muscular waist and rooted around the bathroom for any toiletries. Just like a five-star hotel, they had everything I could ever need. I took a long time brushing my teeth, used the complimentary deodorant and cologne, and even got in a good shave. Needless to say, I felt like a million credits!

While brushing my teeth, which felt so good, I heard soft music piped in through a speaker system somewhere. I wondered if there were any radio stations still broadcasting and if Homestead had ever set up their own station. If Captain Scott's Soul Man still operated, it would pick up any operating stations, which Homestead could use to guide other sleepers and shelties to safety.

Thoroughly clean and feeling fresh, I reminisced about my folks back home in Aurora--well, back home, over 150 years ago. I pondered what had happened to those that actually survived the war. I was sure some people had to have lived through the attacks. It made me think about how bad Denver, Colorado, might have been hit in the Great Destruction and I felt a pang of homesickness.

One Dead Marine

5

THE OATH

Between dream and reality, there's a fine line in many a man's mind...but when you end up in a world that seems to flow right out of the pages of some fantasy novel, you begin to question your very sanity. Lately, even my waking hours are haunted with things I can't explain and even worse, don't want to explain. Have the horrors of our modern life finally caught up with us? I assume, it must have been very easy for my distant, American Indian ancestors to survive in a world where the worst predator was man and the biggest monsters were the grazing buffalo.

~ Tony Moon

One Dead Marine

Dressed only in a towel, I gave the quarters a good once over. I found a clean t-shirt and boxers that fit well along with a very unflattering gray jumpsuit. I threw on the clean clothes, my belt, my wristwatch, and my leather boots. After a quick shine, the boots looked better than the shoes that I found in the room. Dressed and feeling comfortable, I still had time to check out what else was in the room.

The most notable item I found was a video entertainment system complete with a jack for transferring files to and from a Soul Man. It was too bad that I didn't have one on me, because the shelter had a pretty impressive collection of adult films and all were free.

Using the system, I found an information page that highlighted the dinner menu and an extensive Discovery Channel-style directory filled with what was now ancient history.

I had noticed that no one in the shelter, aside from the few guards, carried any weapons around with them and decided to leave all my other gear in the room. I suspected that if they had wanted to take my stuff, they would have done it by now, and I didn't think it would be too cool walking around Homestead with Leadhead's axe strapped to my back.

Sergeant Crash arrived at the appointed time and I noted that he wasn't armed anymore either. That pretty much told me it was the right decision to leave my weapons behind. Across the hall, we buzzed Jessica's door and she answered wearing a similar gray jumpsuit to ours, but was by far better looking than the two of us. It was obvious that she had taken full advantage of all the room's amenities. It almost looked as if Jessica's jumpsuit was made to fit, especially in the right places, which she had quite a lot of.

Sergeant Crash led us to the cafeteria-style dining facility and I had to let Jessica go first. She was so hungry, I was afraid she might try to eat my arm off if I didn't step aside.

I took my time and talked to one of the servers whose name was Rick. He looked like a military wannabe. We joked a bit about zombie meat, which really wasn't much of a joke, but what the hell. I made sure I got a little of everything they had to offer on the menu and then covered the whole pile in gravy.

When I pushed through the doors into the main dining hall, I was a bit taken aback at the size of the room and number of people eating there. At least 150 people filled the dining hall and the faint background music, piped in over the speaker system, was practically drowned out by the multitude of conversations. It was very refreshing to see so many people comfortably eating and enjoying themselves in this crazy world.

I noticed Jessica waving me over to her table and I went to sit down across from her. She was already well on her way to enjoying her meal to the point that she had a little gravy running down her chin.

She started to say something, but I held up my hand to stop her. I placed my fingers along the side of her face and with my thumb I deftly wiped the gravy from her chin. It seemed like a pretty sexy thing to do at the time.

Sergeant Crash plopped down next to us just as Jessica jumped up to get us something to drink--what Rick referred to as "Bug Juice," but looked pretty much like Kool-Aid.

A redheaded guy in a lab coat sat down next to me and asked if I was the "new-guy-recruit."

Sergeant Crash spoke up before I could answer. "Not yet, he hasn't taken the oath yet."

This redheaded guy then told me if I took the oath and joined Homestead, I should come see him. He ended the conversation by adding, "I'll have a job for you." He never told me his name before he left and he seemed a little weird to me.

Sergeant Crash told me not to pay any attention to him. Crash told me he was only looking for someone to scavenge magical ingredients for some work he was doing in researching magic and where it comes from. Crash did add that the guy had a pretty big budget and working for him could be lucrative.

It seemed like Sergeant Crash didn't approve of this newcomer, so I didn't say anything, but I did plan to talk to the guy when I had the chance.

Jessica returned as Sergeant Crash continued. "The shelter really wants you to join up. They're really impressed with you."

I was willing to give my life for them; it wasn't too much of a surprise that they were impressed.

The Oath

Over the course of dinner, I found out Captain Scott was a psychiatrist--again, not a surprise. Crash didn't know too much about her though.

In talking to the good sergeant, I found out that the shelter had some limited success developing a form of zombie repellant that masks your "scent" to their detection ability. They had a prototype, but it didn't last long enough to be very effective except for short uses.

Crishowski told me the big mosquitoes I fought at Veto Slako's gulag were called "Skeeters" and they were all over the Everglades. The bigger ones normally traveled alone and were easier to kill because they were slow. He seemed really interested when I told him about the bug repellant I used against the ones I fought.

I found out the Homestead Oath was much like the U.S. Military's Oath of Enlistment that I took when I enlisted in the Marines. Theirs was just focused on aligning one to Homestead versus America.

I asked more about the surrounding area and Sergeant Crash told me about Avalon, which was a city to the west in the Everglades, built entirely of living matter and old-world junk. He told me that the dragons that Throm pointed out were in actuality big, scaly, flying, fire-breathing lizards. They were not going on my "must-see" list. It seemed as if there were all manner of fantasy creatures, like those I read about in books and saw in the movies. When I asked about Demons, not only did Crash say they, or something like them, existed, but he said it was probably humanity's fault they existed. They seemed to be entering through ancient transporters that were still active. Crash shared that one of the major focuses of Homestead, aside from dealing with the Fool, was to shut down those transporters and stop the flood of demons into the world.

I found out Colonel Jefferies was the officer in charge of Homestead. Both Captain Scott and Sergeant Crash were shelties, not sleepers, and joined the military while growing up and living at Homestead.

After I had bent Crash's ear for a good hour, he decided to leave, again telling me to think about joining Homestead. I had already decided, but I wanted to talk to Jessica about it first before sharing my answer with the sergeant.

Jessica also made a pitch that she might be able to join Homestead's security force, but Sergeant Crash kind of rudely dashed her confidence by asking what background she might have that could possibly help them. I felt her pain when she realized that a marketing executive might not be the most desired skill in the late 2100s.

That was when I decided that we would have to stick together until I was sure she could fend for herself in this strange new world. I knew she had skills that went way beyond her past job title and I aimed to help her discover them.

As Crash was leaving, I jumped up to ask him one more question that I didn't want Jessica to hear. He confirmed for me that vampires, or things like them, did actually exist, but he had never seen one. Crash handed me a communicator that he programmed to his frequency in case I decided to join Homestead.

Jessica and I stayed in the dining hall that night until they literally kicked us out. We talked about what we had learned and this was honestly the longest conversation we had to date. *I liked it.*

In regards to the demon issue, based on our discussions, she had come to the same realization I had. Jessica told me about a study that Heliogistics had done on transporter usage and, based on what she knew, when the Great Destruction occurred, there would have been about 10,000 people in transport status. With that in mind, we realized that could mean there were potentially 10,000 demons either in the demon dimension or now on Earth. Of course, in retrospect, that was across the entire globe and I doubted that many had actually found their way out of the dimension as of yet. Of course, I could have been way wrong on that assumption.

Then, the topic of Bradley came up. It was obvious to me that this woman was still very much in love with her husband, alive or dead, and she would have to get over that if anything were to happen between us. I certainly didn't want to hurt her, or just be the rebound guy. I confessed to her my concerns about him possibly becoming a vampire, especially considering what Sergeant Crash just told me. She had already come to that same conclusion, but I think she was just too afraid to admit it. She told me that was exactly what she thought they looked like--vampires.

Jessica wanted to blame everything on Monica, the girl he was doing when she walked in on them. Granted, it did seem a bit odd that this Monica would be involved and I even suggested that maybe she wanted Jessica to see them having sex. Deep down I thought her love for her husband was clouding her judgment. It seemed obvious that she left him because he was acting weird and he did know she was coming to Monica's house, as did Monica, so I suspect there was more to the story than met the eye.

That was when I dropped the bomb on Jessica and told her that I thought it was also possible that he could still be alive. She immediately decided that we had to find him and save him from whatever he had become.

Again, it was obvious that she still loved him very much and would grab at any straw to have him back. I finally calmed her down and told her we would try to find out what we could, but these were only fantastic conclusions we were dreaming up and for all intents and purposes he probably died in the Great Destruction. I was thinking that if Bradley was indeed a vampire, then he might as well be dead. That seemed to calm her, but I suspected she would have nightmares that night.

After Jessica calmed down, I proposed that she could become very useful to Homestead. Since sleepers were just waking up, I mentioned that her skills in marketing and advertising might be useful in helping the wayward people find Homestead. I didn't have much time to explain my idea, but I had trained with some psychological operations folks in the Marines and they were pretty much just highly-paid, military spin-doctors. I reasoned that if we were going to restore order in this chaotic world, we were going to need a really good media campaign to back us up. Plus, I bet her that her technical skills were better than Crash gave her credit for. I also told her that anyone that knew Heliogistics and had the ability to hack computers would be a great asset to Homestead and maybe me.

Before we left the dining hall, we both decided it would probably be best for me to join Homestead and for us to stay there. I was concerned about her and that we wouldn't have such nice rooms once I joined up but I had pretty much made up my mind by now. I didn't tell her my concerns though as I walked her back to her room.

She thanked me for everything and gave me a sweet kiss on the cheek.

Needless to say, I wasn't ready to go to my bed after that show of affection, so I walked around for a while and saw some lounge areas and barracks that appeared to house a student-like population.

I found what appeared to be another entrance to the shelter but I didn't mess with it. I also ran into a restricted area, but there again I decided it was best to keep my nose clean and stay away. Nothing, so far, had given me cause to distrust the people of Homestead, so

I didn't want to do anything that would make them distrust me.

I easily made my way back to my room, stripped, and had one of the best night's sleep of my life!

*****

My internal watch went off the next morning with enough time for me to still get a quick workout in and some chow for an early breakfast. I threw on some clothes, splashed some water on my face, and bounded out the door and across the hall to see if Jessica would like to join me.

She opened the door all sleepy-eyed and wearing only her panties and bra. Even in her sleep-induced state, she definitely was a sight to see.

Of course, she didn't want to join me, so I dashed off on my own. I piled up again with a great southern-style breakfast and found Sergeant Crash and two other military-types eating in the hall so I joined them.

One of the two with Crash was a Marine Gunnery Sergeant, whose name was Schlotsky. I don't remember the other sergeant's name. The Gunny was a sleeper like me--he bought a pod after his commanding officer released them all from their base. He said he entered stasis about eight months before the Great Destruction and told me his sleeper pod ended up being buried under a swamp. He almost drowned when he was revived.

The Oath

After we ate, I told them all that I had decided to take the oath and join Homestead.

They seemed quite excited and the Gunny let me know they planned to promote me and he wanted me to wear his Corporal stripes. I thought that was pretty cool. I would have liked Jessica to be there, but I knew she was tired and this really was my time, so I let her sleep. I figured she might have been a bit pissed at me later, but she would get over it.

They took me into the restricted area that I saw last night and inside was a huge salt-water holding tank with two massive sharks in it. This tank was part of their water purification process and someone named the Overseer added the sharks as a quirk. This was the first time I had heard about anyone named "Overseer" and didn't have a clue who that was.

They took me to what was clearly an important office. A full-bird Colonel entered from a back room and everyone, including me, snapped quickly to attention. He greeted me politely as Colonel Jefferies and seemed nice enough. I finally knew why the military had adopted Marine ranks--this Jefferies was a true Marine Colonel.

In a quick ceremony, I recited the oath, which was quite similar to the United States Oath of Enlistment, except for a reference to the Overseer versus the President of the United States. Again, I still didn't know who this Overseer was. There was also a reference to obeying the rules and laws of Homestead, which I didn't know, but figured I would find out pretty soon.

With that, the Colonel congratulated me and then promoted me to Corporal. At that point I was wondering just what it took to actually get promoted in Homestead. I was thinking that I probably had more military training than most of the recruits in the shelter, being as I was from the past and not the current time. I did admit, I had nowhere near the experience that the Colonel and Gunny had, but I was sure I was more militarily-skilled than Captain Scott or Sergeant Crash and there should be some stock put in that. I wasn't even sure how much difference the ranks actually made yet, so I decided not to concern myself with it.

After the swearing in and pinning on of rank, the three NCOs took me to a lounge area and the Gunny brought out a fine bottle of liquor, which we all proceeded to slam down. It was still pretty early in the morning, but it was a nice cap to the event. I was kind of surprised that these guys would be this excited about me joining up with Homestead, but the euphoric effects of the alcohol soon washed away any concerns.

I do remember, before I got too drunk, being told to see Staff Sergeant Long about getting outfitted with some basic gear.

After we all stumbled off, I wanted to do a bunch of things right away, like go tell Jessica what I did, go see Staff Sergeant Long and get outfitted, find out about the rank system, see where I would live, but in the end, I wound up passed out in my room.

* * * * *

The Oath

I know there were a million things I wanted to do
and a ton of questions I still wanted to ask, but in my
drunken stupor my mind came to the conclusion that I
needed to do five things first.

Of course, I needed to tell Jessica what I did. After I
sobered up, of course. I didn't want to approach her
drunk like I was as I probably would have made a pass
at her and that would only have ended up bad.

Pretty quick, I needed to find out what the rules and
laws of Homestead were so I didn't accidentally violate
any of them.

This mysterious Overseer was nagging at me. I
needed to find out who he or she was. I had a crazy
drunken thought that it would be horrible if he turned
out to be Bradley, Jessica's husband. I still wonder how
I came up with that crazy thought.

I also needed to find out where Jessica would stay
now, since we were kind of a package deal. I know
wherever we ended up wouldn't be as nice as these
rooms. Since I was just a Corporal in Homestead that
probably wouldn't rate too much on the
accommodation scale; however, I suspected that put
me on a higher scale than others in the shelter. Plus, I
was wondering if they would actually give us separate
quarters. It seemed obvious that Sergeant Crash
thought Jessica and I were here as a couple and that
wasn't the case.

Lastly, I needed to get with Staff Sergeant Long and
find out what kind of outfitting I would get. I know I

had a pretty effective axe that belonged to Leadhead, but the revolver I was carrying just wasn't going to cut it. The shield I had was a bit heavy and a poly plate one would be better because it could be bigger.

I had used a compound bow before and I suspected that arrows were cheaper and easier to find than ammunition, so it might be good to try to get one of those. I used to have a really good heavy compound bow with optical sights that I used in competitions. I knew they could be pretty effective and particularly silent.

A good assault rifle like the one Crash had would be nice but I'd really like to get my hands on a good assault shotgun and a sweet, scoped-out, sniper rifle. Those would all be good weapons when dealing with zombies and skeeters.

As I was drunkenly dreaming of the weapons I wanted, I figured Homestead could throw in a really nice semi-automatic side arm with a high load capacity, a laser scope, and refined rifling.

I realized that I was going to also need some armor...poly plate preferably or lighter...I didn't want to end up hindered in something heavy and bulky. I never really liked working in heavy armor and I doubted powered armor would be too effective out in the Everglades.

With the amount of things I was running into, I was definitely going to need to get some good equipment like Stichpacks, rations, a pack, and other like items. I suspected the really techie stuff like Nods and a Soul Man were difficult to come by, but I really didn't know.

Once I feel asleep, I had a really weird dream that I used a magic marker to name my three rocks "Menie," "Mini," and "Moe." Then I labeled my impoverished sling "Joe" and hung them all above my fireplace mantel. It was odd, since I had no idea where I was, or why I would do that, but I clearly remember doing it.

Aside for a hefty hangover, I really looked forward to waking up!

6

FLORIDA CITY

Time, defined by the dictionary is a number or interval, representing a specific point on the continuum, sometimes listed as a span of years, marked by similar events, conditions, or phenomena; an apparently irreversible succession from the past through the present to the future. Among the Indian peoples of North America, history is far more a matter of Place than of Time. Rather than dates and events, the sense is: Here, in this sacred place, something important happened long ago that we remember in story and ritual generation after generation. When it happened is not very significant. Where it happened is what matters. The land shapes us and tells our history rather than the other way around. In this framework, Time is viewed, not as linear, but rather as cyclical. The American Indian views time through the lens of the land and how the seasons weave through the land's story. Everything begins and ends with the land.

~Tony Moon

It was almost 1300 when I woke up with only a slight headache. The first thing I did was reset my watch to the current date and time displayed on the in-room video.

It was Sunday, 8 May 2196, only five days to Friday the 13th. Not a day I was looking forward to, but every day in this world seemed like Friday the 13th.

I threw on my clothes and hurried to the chow hall to grab a bite before they closed up. I got a great sandwich, but kept it kind of light since I had been packing on the carbs and hadn't really been working out. I wondered if they had a gym at Homestead.

That was when Sergeant Crash beeped me on the communicator and asked me to come to his office. He already had a mission for me--nothing like getting settled.

I reminded him that I had only been in Homestead all of one day and a half and I had no clue where his office was.

He directed me back to the secure area by Colonel Jefferies office.

I then reminded him that I didn't have access to that area.

He realized his error and told me he had my key card in his hand. I was thinking that either Sergeant Crash wasn't working with a full deck or he was still drunk. Both I supposed could have been possible.

That was when the brainiac realized he would have to bring me the key card before I could come to see him. Up to this point, my head wasn't really hurting, but I could feel a "stupid headache" coming on.

I once had a dog that I had tied up in front of my house near the front door. Because the dog was tied up near the mailbox, the postman refused to deliver mail to my house. So, the post office sent me a letter in the mail telling me the Postman refused to deliver my mail until I moved my dog. I occurred to me that one of Crash's ancestors must have worked at that post office.

Crash told me he would meet me at the door to the restricted area so I finished eating. That seemed to make the cleaning crew happy as they were waiting on me again.

Sergeant Crash was waiting for me by the entrance. He handed me the key card to the restricted area of the compound and we went back to his office where he briefed me on the details of my first mission with Homestead.

Turns out they wanted me to go to some place called Florida City--I had no clue where that was. He explained Florida City was an agricultural compound in a big park, where Homestead grew food for the shelter. Over the past two weeks, five people had gone missing. Around here that didn't seem too odd to me, but they wanted me to investigate it. I figured it might be the Fool, but they didn't think he was behind this. They figured if he knew about Florida City he would have attacked them already and not taken them out one by one.

Sergeant Crash didn't have much information to go on regarding the problem so my instructions were to go to Florida City and meet with the civilian supervisor, Mr. John Freeman. During the mission briefing, I had to actually ask what the supervisor's name was. I guess Crash just assumed I would know.

I asked for and received a map of Southern Florida from Sergeant Crash. I couldn't understand why he thought I knew so much more than I did. When he told me I should get a Soul Man, I asked if they were issued, to which he answered "No." At that point I expected him to tell me I needed to get a better weapon next. This guy was clearly not helpful or bright.

When Crash was done with his mission brief, he directed me to go see Staff Sergeant Long to get equipped.

Since I didn't know anything about Homestead, I had to ask where I could find Staff Sergeant Long. I also asked what else was available to Jessica and I in Homestead and where it was.

As it turned out there was a whole section of the shelter dedicated to schools and shops with the Individual Equipment Issue at the far end of that section. That explained the student dormitories I saw the night before. Crash rattled off that they had an inn, a factory, an artisan shop, a bakery, a workshop, an ammo and explosives store, a craftsman store, a couple of clothing stores, and a survival store. Additionally, Homestead had everything the military needed--a combat simulator, which I had experienced firsthand, weapons and armor stores, a communications and computer store, and medical and provision supply stores. The shelter also provided technology, medical, and vehicle operations schools on the premises.

He told me that I would receive free food and lodging and get paid 1,000 credits a month, plus applicable bonuses, for working for the shelter. He confirmed that pay was based on my rank but he didn't say what each rank made or what it took to make rank around the shelter.

I had to pump this guy for information and he acted like everyone new to Homestead got an information pamphlet or something. I wasn't trying to sound rude, but I had to ask another rather critical question, "Where are Jessica and I to move to?"

The sergeant told me that Homestead was setting up a facility for us, which would have two bedrooms and basic furniture, but it wouldn't be ready for a few days. He told me I would need to buy some stuff to spruce up the quarters since it would be really sparse. That was a nice way of saying that I was getting low rent housing.

I was amazed that he thought I had any money on me when he knew how we ended up here. I'd hoped they would at least provide us the basic provisions like a few changes of clothes, toiletries, etc. However, at this point, it was looking like Homestead was a "fend for yourself" shelter, much like life on the outside. At least the shelter provided safety for us, which I was thinking was pretty important at the moment.

I hid my impatience with Sergeant Crash pretty well. The whole time I thought he didn't have a clue as to our current situation, but I asked my questions without much emotion through the entire conversation.

I questioned Crash on what rules we were expected to follow since I had taken an oath to uphold them, but didn't know what they were. He handed me a big red book that was about 500 pages, which turned out to basically be the Uniform Code of Military Justice, and everyone in Homestead was expected to follow it.

That made things a bit easier, even though I thought the code would be a bit too restrictive for a civilian and student population, like the one in Homestead.

I thought it best to explain my relationship with Jessica. Crash told me that she could live in the shelter as my dependant even though we were not attached. He said, since the place I was getting was a two-bedroom, she should have no problem living there.

I mentioned Jessica's media skills and her desire to support the shelter like I was.

He said he would have some folks in Shelter Publicity, their closed-circuit system, contact her about possible work. That made me feel good.

The conversation shifted to how my communicator actually worked. It turned out I needed to load people's communicator codes into it in order to actually contact them. He gave me the codes to Homestead Control, Homestead Security, Florida City, and Mr. Freeman. It was a good thing I asked about that.

Florida City

Crash told me to check in when I thought it was important and that I officially would be working in Special Operations. He said that they put me in that section because of my background and that I probably would operate out of that section for a while. That sounded pretty good to me.

I left the office and headed back to my room feeling as if there was a lot I still didn't know. If someone is new to this entire world, there really should be a little better briefing about what is going on and what one needs to do. I still really wasn't sure what all I needed to do in Homestead to get ready for this mission.

It felt like no one even realized that we both just woke up in this world about a month ago and escaped the Great Destruction by mere minutes over 150 years ago. Crash clearly was not a student of the obvious and what made it worse was that I would be working for this guy.

When I got to my room, I grabbed all my stuff and proceeded down to Equipment Issue.

Homestead was sending me out all alone into a hostile environment to investigate something I knew nothing about and to a place I had never even heard of. It sounded a little like being Special Forces that were air-dropped into a new war zone.

I wasn't overly impressed with Equipment Issue either. Sergeant Long gave me a simple uniform, a canvas backpack, a couple of one-liter canteens, seven rations, a single-shot, magazine-fed rifle, two 15-round

93

magazines with basic ammo, a very simple Poly Plate helmet, and Poly Plate breast piece.

Turns out that Long traded some too, so I turned in the skeleton's big battle axe, my empty revolver, some brass shell casings, and other little items I picked up for some coin. At least here I felt like I had received a fairer deal on trade than at the outpost weeks ago. Maybe I was getting better at the barter game or being in Homestead made it better--the answer was probably a little of both.

On one hand, I was happy they gave me anything at all, but on the other, I was a bit surprised that this was all I was issued. I probably should have asked for other things, but I was still a bit stunned by the whole attitude that I faced so far. My gut told me that this limited equipment issue would come back to haunt me later, or maybe even kill me.

My mom used to say not to look a gift horse in the mouth, but she also said to never look it in the butt either as it might kick you in the head! I was thinking I was about to stand behind one hell of a gift horse.

I went directly to find Jessica to break the good news to her and found her in the dining hall with two other women. Turns out she had already made some friends named June and Gail. They told me she had done nothing but talk about me all day long. At least she was meeting women and not other men.

I broke the news to Jessica about signing up, which she took pretty well, but she certainly wasn't happy about me going to Florida City. She actually thought I would have been pulling guard duty or something boring like that.

I promised her that I would be back soon and there was nothing to worry about. I hoped I was a pretty convincing liar, because at that point I wasn't very sure about any of it.

My positive attitude about the situation seemed to console her and we walked together back to my room where I dumped what gear I wasn't going to take on the mission. I found the equipment they had given me plus what I still owned was so heavy that it slowed me down. Once I sorted everything I would take and stored it in the pack on my back, I was able to handle it well enough.

Jessica walked me all the way to the airlock, which kind of bugged me. I hated saying goodbye to her as it was and that made for a really long walk.

We said our goodbyes and I gave her a quick kiss on the cheek with a mischievous wink. As I hugged her, she seemed more confident that I wasn't being as much of a fool as I thought I was, leaving like that. I guess it was a good thing I didn't tell her I was going alone.

Once top-side, I pulled out my map and realized, for the first time, that I had no clue where I was going or how I would get there. It would have been nice to have that covered in the briefing. I figured I would just have to walk.

Florida City was to the southwest of Homestead, which was the opposite direction of the Fool and that provided me some relief.

I looked around the perimeter, which was guarded by large wooden towers and each was manned with one of those large pulse cannons I had seen when I arrived. Between each tower was an energy wall of some type. I figured I would just have to walk up to one section and ask to pass through.

As I was about to probably make a huge mistake, a Private First Class Joe came running up to me. He told me he had been waiting for me and that he worked in the motor pool. He was supposed to help me requisition a motorcycle for the mission.

No one had bothered to ask, so I had to tell him that I had never operated a motorcycle before.

He recommended I go to Vehicle Ops School to learn how to ride one.

While I thought that was a great suggestion, it was about 150 years too late. I explained that I needed to get to Florida City right away and didn't have time to learn how to ride a motorcycle.

He asked if I would like him to order up a "pickup," to which I responded positively.

I could definitely drive one of those. I was grateful but still had no clue what to expect.

The "pickup" turned out to be a very quiet helicopter run on power cells. I had expected a vehicle with four tires and an open bed but climbed aboard ready to head to Florida City.

The pilot expected me to hook up the communications system to my helmet but it was a very basic helmet without that capability so he opted for communication with hand signals, which worked fine.

I just hoped he didn't have anything important to say to me on the trip over.

We flew over the jungles that surrounded Florida City and I couldn't see any obvious signs of a roadway or civilization. I wondered what went through Sergeant Crash's head that he would expect me to be able to make it to this place on a motorcycle. Traveling on foot would have been even more ludicrous!

As I reviewed the events leading up to the mission, I began to wonder if Sergeant Crash purposely set me up to fail on this mission. Then I thought maybe he was just as dumb as I was naïve.

*****

After about 20 minutes of flying over the Hell that used to be Florida, we came in on a low bank over the agricultural compound. I think the pilot might have been trying to make me puke, but I spent enough time in the back of helicopters during my Marine training that the flight didn't even phase me. I noticed recent plantings in the growing area of the compound which was basically a large square of open area surrounded on all sides by jungle. The heat there was even more oppressive than outside Homestead.

As we landed in the compound, two guards came out to greet me and I introduced myself. I wanted to go see

Mr. John Freeman immediately and get started on my investigation right away.

The two guards escorted me to Freeman's quarters which were pretty bare. He was a plain-looking man. I guessed he was in his mid-thirties.

I introduced myself as Corporal Anthony Moon from Homestead and he seemed relieved that Homestead finally sent someone out to help. I started with some questions about what was going on.

The first worker to disappear, Jessi Black, occurred about two weeks ago--27 Apr 2196. She had disappeared without any sign and everyone just assumed it was a random monster.

After Jessi, other members of the community started disappearing and they realized it was more than a random occurrence and not coincidence.

According to Freeman, nobody ever witnessed the abductions and the victims were always alone when it happened.

I asked if he had warned everyone in the compound to only travel in groups of two or more and he assured me he instituted that policy two nights ago, but the last one to disappear, Jeremy West, was young and wasn't following the rules when he went to the latrine alone. He was lost on the 6th of May.

I looked around and noticed there wasn't anyone else in Mr. Freeman's office. I asked him what his excuse was for not following his own policy.

His eyes darted around nervously and then I watched the light bulb go on in his head. The growing redness of his cheeks showed his embarrassment.

I told him that by not following his own policy, he I was sending a non-verbal message to the rest of the compound that it wasn't important enough to follow.

He told me he would rectify that immediately.

I asked if he could assign someone to stay with me while I was conducting the investigation so it didn't look like I was ignoring the policy as well. I figured I could use a guide in and around the compound anyway.

John hooked me up with a guy named Steve as my escort.

We went over who the other victims were and whether they had anything in common that might have made them targets.

The other missing were Charlie Jones, who went to the latrine alone, James Jolly, who was out playing alone, and Susan Rogers, who was simply running from one tent to another.

The walk from the camp to the latrine was about 30 yards from the camp circle. John Freeman told me they kept a large fire in the center of the camp at all times. During the day, the fire pit was just hot embers but at night they keep it burning to provide light. Unfortunately, the light provided by the fire was pretty limited around the compound and really didn't illuminate well to the latrine.

I couldn't find any specific pattern amongst the victims through our discussion, so I changed my course of questioning. I asked if anything out of the ordinary had happened before the disappearances started.

John told me that aside from a regular family rotation on the 24th nothing odd or different had happened. Both of the families that rotated in and out had lived and worked in the compound several times before.

My escort, Steve, arrived and I decided to do a little investigating on my own.

First, I went to speak with Rick Black, Jessi Black's husband.

The last time he had seen her, she was at the campfire when he went to bed. She never came home that night. He told me he and Jessi hadn't been getting along too well but said he wouldn't want anything to happen to her. He also informed me they had a son there as well.

When I pressed him to remember if there was anything else about that night, he did have something odd to add.

He had found a vial by their tent the next morning. He picked the vial up off a table and handed it to me. It was unlabeled, but there was a small amount of residue in the bottom of it.

He mentioned they all were scheduled to rotate back to Homestead on the 22nd, but he wanted to stay until his wife was found.

Thanking him, I took the vial to Mr. Freeman and asked him to examine the residue.

Oddly, Freeman had known about the vial, but assumed it was unrelated.

It seemed pretty important to me so he complied.

He told me it would take about four hours to examine the contents.

I decided to go scope out the area between the fire pit and the Black's tent while I was waiting, to see if I could find anything else out of the ordinary.

The camp was so full of junk that someone could stalk up and jump anyone in the dark without ever being seen. Behind a woodpile, by the Black's tent, Steve and I found a perfect hiding spot amongst all the piles of junk.

In that spot, Steve discovered a cork lying on the ground. The cork looked a perfect fit for the vial Rick had given me earlier, so I pocketed it to check later.

There by the tent was a large maul lying on a stump. I thought it was worth noting that if someone was hidden there, they obviously didn't need this weapon and left it behind.

Steve and I went next to check out Charlie Jones and Jeremy West's last known locations.

I couldn't help but notice a pile of tires with a great hiding place in the center right by where they were both abducted. This proved a perfect place to hide between the tents and the latrine.

After a little investigation of that area, we found three things.

First was some broken glass on the ground that looked like the remains of another vial. I gathered up the remnants in hopes that we could compare any possible residue on the glass to the other vial.

Secondly, there were some boot prints in the center of the tires, which at least meant that we weren't the only ones to find this spot.

Lastly, Steve and I found what looked like drag marks from the path between Jeremy West's tent and the tires. It looked like someone might have dragged someone or something into the hiding spot in the tire pile.

By this time it had been four hours, so Steve and I returned to talk with Mr. Freeman.

It turned out that the residue in the vial had traces of rare chemical parts, which were commonly used for a drug or potion. Also, there were other compounds found in the vial, which had Freeman guessing it could have contained some kind of poison, radiation barrier draught, or something similar.

I told him I suspected it to be a knock out poison of some type. I pulled the cork and smashed bits of vial from my pocket and asked him to check to see if they exuded the same signatures.

I let him know about our recent discoveries and told him that based on the hiding spots and drag marks, I definitely suspected a human or humanoid presence at work there. I hypothesized that there was someone knocking people out, or killing them, from the cover of the junk in the camp and then dragging them off to their hiding spot and then possibly carrying them off somewhere else.

Freeman suggested we check around the edge of the compound. He told us that there was a path that led into the swamp where the ground was soft. Normally no one goes into the swamp and if people were being carried out that way we might find good footprints there.

Glancing out the window, I noticed that it was getting dark and I didn't want to try anything in the swamp in the dark. I decided that our investigation there would have to wait until the next day. In the meantime, I needed to impress upon everyone in the camp the importance of staying in groups of two or more while I continued my investigation.

Freeman felt that it would have more impact if I were to speak to them myself. He thought it would carry more weight if the message came from me as the primary investigator. Since it was almost dinner time in the compound, Freeman was willing to gather everyone for me to speak to them.

I agreed with his idea and Steve and I went with him and his escort to the center of the camp. There he assembled everyone except the guards in the towers around the camp.

I explained the situation and impressed upon them the need to travel in groups. There were a few questions, but the announcement and my presence there in the camp seemed to settle everyone's fears.

That night, Steve and I set up shop in Freeman's office. When it got dark, I decided to do a little scouting with Steve. After adjusting our eyes to night vision by sitting in the dark for half an hour, we headed out into the camp. Moving around the outer ring of the camp, it became clear that even a non-stealthy invader like Steve could move about undetected. With the limited firelight, the excessive junk, and jungle noises in the background, anyone could come and go as they pleased.

We decided to stake out in the tires we checked out earlier and watched the jungle entrance Mr. Freeman spoke of that afternoon.

By 0100, the camp had become quite silent, so we went back to the office. Thus far, everyone had been abducted around the hours of 2100 to 2200 and we figured if anything was going to happen, it would have by then.

The next morning I sent Steve back to check up on his family while I worked with Mr. Freeman. The first thing we did was have everyone in the camp clear all the junk away and move it to the outer edge of the camp. This opened up the camp considerably and would make it very difficult for anyone to hide.

I had Freeman establish a two-person roving patrol in the camp at night until we figured out who or what was behind these abductions. Up to this point, all they had were guards in the towers that ringed the edge of the compound, but no one inside the camp itself.

Lastly, I instituted a daily roll call so anyone who went missing would be noticed right away.

Freeman and I then went to check out the edge of the camp in the early daylight hours. Sure enough, we not only found one set of tracks, but two. They were odd tracks; shorter and wider than my feet and with a pattern that suggested the wearing of really crude leather foot coverings. It also looked like they were carrying something between the two of them by the weight and way they were walking.

I called in the situation to Sergeant Crash relaying everything I had learned and was doing. He said he would send some lighting devices to help with the camp security.

Mr. Freeman and I returned to his office and sat down to talk about plans. I instructed him on setting up an ambush if the two invaders returned, an act that might save my life as I was planning to go into the swamp to see if I could find the missing people. The quicker we found the missing, the better chance they would have of being alive so I was worried about waiting too long.

I gave Freeman some quick instructions on how to employ the lighting that was on its way from Homestead so the camp could still remain undetected at night. I didn't think it would be a good idea to light up the sky and alert the Fool to their position.

Freeman warned me about potential creatures I might encounter in the swamp. He told me about nipplings, bad apples, and skeeters that were in the swamps around the compound. I knew what skeeters were and hoped that I wouldn't run into any of them.

As we were discussed the local area, he also told me about a place nearby called Flamingo, which was an Elf city. He shared with me a recent visit they had from a Sorcerer and two explorers that came from Everglade City to the west, which was a really big free town that had not been hit by the Great Destruction.

I found all his information fascinating, but it had little impact on the current investigation.

Steve volunteered to join me on my expedition. I sent him off to tell his family that he had volunteered. I also made sure Mr. Freeman understood that Steve was volunteering and would be duly recognized for the act. When Steve returned, we borrowed a lantern, first aid kit, and compass from Mr. Freeman. Then, at mid-day, we struck off into the swamp, following the tracks.

*****

We followed the tracks into the swamp for a bit when we came upon a skeeter that Steve called huge. I actually dropped it really quick with some well-aimed shots from my rifle. Unfortunately, two more skeeters must have heard the shots as they came flying into view--these were much smaller, like the ones that I had fought before. I decided to switch weapons, based on guidance earlier, and wait for them to come within striking range. I found that smashing these in the torso with a good weapon was very effective.

Steve got hurt a bit in the fight, but did very well against them--he certainly was invaluable. I told him to return to the camp though because he was pretty banged up and I was good so far.

As I pressed on, I caught sight of an even smaller flying-thing zipping behind a tree. I waited it out and soon got to see my first nippling. It was a very small and ugly impish-looking creature. He had a tiny bow and zipped in to take his first shot at me, which bounced off my shield. He screamed something at me about his race replacing humans, which sounded odd and very evil.

I saw that the arrow he used was coated with something, so I decided I needed to take immediate action. Switching weapons, I waded in with my fire axe. Although he was hard to hit, I pressed him hard. He was slow to reload and I think I was able to really scare him...so much so that he decided I was more of a danger than he expected and he fled into the swamp. I was a little worried I might see him again with some of his buddies next time.

A while later I happened upon the biggest skeeter I had seen so far. The pest was practically the size of a horse. That made me think about my "gift horse" thought the day earlier. We beat on each other for a while before I was able to kill it, but it really knocked me around. My cheap armor proved only slightly effective against its huge--no, enormous--stinger.

After I dispatched it, I realized I must have turned wrong somewhere in the swamp as I couldn't find the tracks anymore. I must have been watching my back too much after the nippling incident, fearing he might return. I turned around, found the tracks again and, was back on the right track.

Once I got back on the trail, I came upon a half-sunken house in the swamp. I thought it best to radio in my position before I tried to go in the house.

I realized that I let Steve keep the lantern when he left, which was a pretty stupid move--the house was dark inside. That made me wish they had at least issued me some type of light source. I crafted a torch to use.

Once the torch was lit, I moved toward the house by crossing a stone bridge of sorts. I spotted two red eyes momentarily in the darkness of the house's entrance. Suddenly a laser fired out of the house, which I deflected just in time with my shield.

Without thinking, I charged into the open front door of the house. In retrospect, this was probably a pretty dumb move on my part, but normally what I lacked in brains I made up for in brawn. As I charged into the house to confront my aggressors, I could sense there were two of them.

What I saw burned in my memory forever. Inside were two pale-white albino creatures with red wickedly-glowing eyes. One was wearing all leather except on his hands and he wielded the laser pistol. A strange device hung from his belt. The other one was really ugly and also wearing full leather armor. In one knobby hand he held a meat cleaver and in the other a bloody carving knife.

As I charged through the doorway, I deftly deflected another laser shot as I dropped my torch to the ground to provide light and free up my weapon hand. I yanked my trusty axe free of its straps and cracked the one with the pistol.

Knowing the other would wade in to attack, I attempted to spin towards him as he committed himself to a wild charge attack. Unfortunately, the floor in the house was all rocky and uneven and I completely missed blocking his deadly cleaver swipe at my left leg.

I almost didn't feel any pain as I tumbled to the ground alongside my severed leg. My Marine training kicked in as I realized that any further aggressive actions on my part would certainly kill me. Fighting back the mounting pain and probable shock due to immediate blood loss, I quickly feigned unconsciousness.

Believing me to be unconscious, the grotesque men roughly bandaged my leg and bound my hands and feet before roughly hoisting me and carrying me through a compartment in the floor and down a ladder.

I suspected that they were taking me into a sleeper pod, but it was so dark I couldn't see a thing. It appeared that they didn't need any light source to effectively move about in the dark.

They dumped me on a cold metal floor and by this time I was pretty positive it was a pod. I lay there trying not to move when I heard a keyboard being used in the darkness. Suddenly there was a "whooshing" noise of a sleeper tube opening with the accompanying computer voice ringing out, "Stasis pod ready."

Then it hit me...they were using the tubes as a meat locker. I realized that they planned to freeze me for a later dinner.

I realized I was pretty much doomed if I didn't do something so I tried to struggle. It was hopeless as they threw me in the tube on top of another cold body and the door slid quickly shut.

I tried to get to my communicator to key the mike...anything...but then the cold hit me and everything went dark.

As the tendrils of the icy cryogenics took hold, my mind screamed. First off, my stupidity probably put got me in this tube. I should have, armchair quarterbacking the situation, waited outside the house in hiding. That would have allowed me the advantage in the situation, but I had to be bold and charge in blindly to an ambush myself.

My freezing mind was grasping at any last hope. Since it had been three days since the camp had seen a visit from these two invaders, chances were they probably would have struck out that night looking for more food for their storage locker. If the creatures went to the camp to pick out another morsel for their freezer they would trigger the ambush that I had set up for them. Then Freeman and his guards might come looking for me.

I had radioed in my position and situation before I went into the house. After a bit, Homestead might actually get worried and send out a search team for me.

Florida City

My final frozen thoughts were of Homestead and Sergeant Crash. I could not believe how poorly I was prepared to take on this mission. I know they didn't know what I would be facing, but even the densest tree in the forest would have realized that sending someone out so poorly armed and equipped with no knowledge of how to get around or what to expect was pretty much suicide.

This all led my mind to one of two conclusions. Sergeant Crash was either an idiot who didn't have any planning or logic skills, or he wanted me to fail on this mission, which I found a bit hard to swallow. Of course, I was an idiot for not requesting more stuff that I should have known I would need and I at least had some clue as what to expect outside Homestead from my previous wanderings.

Darkness...

ABOUT THE SAVAGE SOUL™

The Savage Soul™ is a role-playing game set in a world that incorporates almost every imaginable genre, including fantasy, science fiction, espionage, modern warfare, and horror. As such, it is both a generic role-playing system (suitable for any type of adventure) and a world that offers limitless possibilities for the creative Game Master. In fact, in the course of a single adventure, a *Savage Soul*™ character might find himself casting spells, hacking computers, shooting zombies, slashing at warbots, seducing beauties, gambling in casinos, negotiating with vampires, and performing surgery.

To some Game Masters, this may sound daunting. But *The Savage Soul*™ is as much or as little as you want it to be.   Your initial game setting may be as simple as a wild forest or barren desert, where little technology exists from before "The Great Destruction." On the other hand, your game may be set in the outskirts of a once-thriving metropolis, with certain communities having preserved or restored their high-tech lifestyles (including computer networks, dimensional transporters, and automated surgery centers). Most of the world, however, will likely fall somewhere in between, with small, isolated communities clinging to scraps of technology while simultaneously exploiting the benefits of magic and alchemy.

ABOUT THE AUTHOR

John Knotts is a results-oriented business professional and consultant with twenty years experience working with the military, small businesses, and nonprofits. He is the President of *Crosscutter Enterprises*, which provides business management consulting services, and is the President and Publisher for *SAXtreme Magazine*, which promotes an active and healthy lifestyle in San Antonio, Texas.

John retired from the U.S. Air Force in July 2008 and has worked as an external consultant since. He was born and raised in the Detroit-area of Michigan but now lives in San Antonio, Texas. For those who know the Air Force, he was in the Security (Police) Forces for ten years and then retrained to Manpower and (Quality) Organization and was in that career field for eleven years. He has been stationed at Carswell Air Force Base (AFB), Texas (six years), Vandenberg AFB, California (two years), Turkey (one year), Ramstein Air Base, Germany (six years), and in San Antonio at Lackland AFB (six years).

For John, writing is a passion aligned to his professional and personal life. His interests cover fiction, nonfiction (business), as well as journalism. You can find him online at http://johnrknotts.wordpress.com.

Made in the USA
Columbia, SC
20 June 2023

18416854R00079